Helen Griffiths

THE
WILD HEART

ILLUSTRATED BY VICTOR G. AMBRUS

DOUBLEDAY & COMPANY, INC.

GARDEN CITY, NEW YORK

By the Same Author

HORSE IN THE CLOUDS
WILD AND FREE
MOONLIGHT
AFRICANO

Library of Congress Catalog Card Number 64–11295
Copyright © 1963 by Helen Griffiths
*Illustrations Copyright © 1963 by Hutchinson & Co. (Publishers) **Ltd.***
All Rights Reserved
Printed in the United States of America
First Edition in the United States of America

CONTENTS

Chapter 1

SCARECROW FILLY

I

The gauchos say that there is a heaven for horses. They call it Trapalanda. It is a place of great beauty; fresh and constantly green, with running water that never fails, shady trees, blue skies and warm sun. It is a place where no flies sting, where men are non-existent. Nor are there pumas and wild dogs. Winter never comes to Trapalanda and everywhere is peace.

Angel, often called Ranito, liked to believe that Trapalanda existed, especially when he thought of La Bruja, the mare whose life had been hard until she came almost miraculously into his hands. Perhaps she was there now, filling her belly with luscious grass, dribbling cool water through her lips, kicking up her heels like the filly she once had been, snorting and rubbing noses with Pegaso, who was white and winged and the king of horses. Life could not be so cruel that there was no rest at the end of it.

Angel often thought of La Bruja. She had been a savage brute when she first took shelter with him, yellow teeth constantly ready to tear, nervous hoofs ever alert, and she was named La Bruja—The Witch— because of her disposition. Angel was to know her better nature, but the name stuck because, after all, it was her name.

But the story of La Bruja began long before she came into Angel's keeping and long before she was coveted by man.

It began on the empty pampa when the midday sun was at its zenith in the azure sky and a lone mare sweated below it, straining with the pangs of labor. She had endured many hours thus and the foal was long in coming, seemingly unwilling to leave the dark haven in which it had been succored for so long.

The mare was thirsty but there was no water near. There was grass in plenty—tall, thick grass which obscured her up to the knees—but the grunting animal was not hungry. She labored patiently, passing the long hours staring at the horizon, moving in a slow circle, sometimes sinking down to rest. She did not rest often, a constant fear of danger keeping her alert while she was so helpless.

The horizon was deserted. Grass stretched endlessly about her, touching the sky in the distance, and the green on earth below her hoofs was matched by the blue of the sky above her head, unbroken by a single cloud. She saw no suspicious movement, heard no suspicious sound, and the slight wind that breathed constantly through the grasses brought no scent of danger to her widely distended nostrils. So far she was safe.

Suddenly the mare felt strong movements within her and she knew her time had come. First two tiny hoofs, followed by a quivering nose; a big damp head with flattened ears; neck, shoulders, flanks and haunches, with a straggly bit of tail at the end; an ungainly foal which the mare had long awaited tumbling into the grass.

It was a filly-foal, La Bruja, and the world was dark to her just then, before her eyes could see. There was naught in her world as yet, except perhaps shock and confusion and then a warmth which began slowly stealing over her as the rough tongue of her mother began to stimulate her skin.

She snorted and kicked and trembled. Life was strong within her and the blood began pulsing through her veins in tune with her fast-expanding lungs. A second struggle produced a minor bleat from a mouth newly opened and the flattened ears began to prick, the straggly tail to shake itself and the gangling legs to tremble.

Wild kicks followed as La Bruja fought to find some usage for her legs, and she struggled helplessly on her flank for several minutes, while the mother looked on and licked occasionally, until a sense of balance came to her with an urge to push herself upward.

Her first attempts were failures, but La Bruja was new to the world and did not know when she was beaten. She stretched her legs and forced her weight upon them. At times she forgot to straighten her hoofs first, so that she overbalanced before she could even stand. When she remembered to put her hoofs on the ground first and managed to stand steadily on all four stick-like legs she did not know what to do next. For a moment or two she swayed back and forth, trying to lift one leg and shuffle it forward, and her efforts took time and patience, for more often than not she failed and fell into the grass.

While La Bruja struggled thus, the mare resumed her steady watch of the horizon. Her thirst was greater now and she was anxious to leave the birthplace of the foal, the warm smell of which would travel on the wind and reach the searching nostrils of some hungry hunter, but until the foal had learned to use her legs flight was impossible.

The sun was westward-bound, but the sky was still bright in the east where darkness comes first. The destination of the mare lay in the east, where others of her kind were gathered. When the foal should be fit to travel the mare would seek the company of the herd, and she stared anxiously toward the eastern horizon, waiting on the foal.

La Bruja learned. She had several falls, but surprise was greater than any injury and before much time had passed she was prancing awkwardly around the mare, poking, sniffing and prodding with her rough, large head, hunger the strongest instinct now within her.

The mare stood still and patient, wise to the ways of foals, and after much experimenting, nibbling at her mother's tail, sucking her knees and hocks and belly, La Bruja found the right place. She stood with legs splayed wide apart, neck twisted and tail flicking excitedly, gulping mouthfuls of warm, sweet milk until her skinny belly was bloated and she gasped for breath.

Then the mare grew rougher, for shadows were creeping over the eastern pampa and she was still far from the safety of the herd which awaited her. She pushed the foal aside whenever La Bruja searched again to suck and she began moving slowly toward the herd.

La Bruja stood still, uncomprehending. The mare looked round and nickered a soft command to follow. La Bruja did not understand. She stamped her hoof and bleated angrily, milk still dribbling from her wet, pink jaws, and she flicked her rag of tail.

The mare came back to her and gently nudged her forward, but La Bruja still did not understand. The mare tried again and, pushing with head and breast, sometimes roughly, sometimes gently, she gradually persuaded the foal to come.

In this erratic manner, with La Bruja sometimes bounding ahead and sometimes lagging far behind, staring longingly after the retreating mare, the two of them traveled slowly in the direction of the herd, darkness before them and failing light behind.

Thus were La Bruja's first hours on the pampa.

II

La Bruja was never coveted by any man for her beauty, for she was far from beautiful. Even as a foal, when babyhood lends a natural attractiveness to clumsy figures, La Bruja was ugly.

Her sire was of the Criollo breed and she inherited his roman nose but none of his pride of carriage. Her head was overlarge, held always too high, as if constantly in search of danger, and her ears seemed to be too small in comparison, half hidden in a fuzzy forelock and untidy mane. Her body was long and always skinny. Even though she fed well on her mother's milk there never seemed to be any flesh to cover her bones and, with bloated belly but ribby flanks, she looked more like a scarecrow than a filly-foal.

The length of her legs was amazing, more than that of any other foal in the herd, so that she was taller than all her brothers, and these long legs and long body revealed that she was not pure-blooded and that there was more of her mother's sire in her than her own.

La Bruja's mother was only half Criollo. Her sire was a thoroughbred stallion, newly imported to the land, who, unable to resist the call of freedom which whispered constantly to him through the grass and on the wind, broke away from his master and claimed as his own the first wild mare he found. In the resultant offspring the hardy Criollo blood proved strongest and La Bruja's mother seemed to possess none of the ancient blood of her sire. But in La Bruja, granddaughter of the thoroughbred, nature had reverted itself and she was three parts like her grandsire and only one part native pony.

Her coloring was vague, a sort of liver brown with mottled haunches, and her eyes and nostrils were pink-rimmed, giving her a vicious appearance long before hatred became part of her nature. Her ragged tail and brush-like mane were of a gingery tone and, all in all, she looked as though she had been thrown together in a hurry with no particular care being taken to see that all the parts fitted or matched.

But though so ugly, she was healthy and strong and for a wild horse there is nothing more important than these two things. The wild horse has little cunning, therefore it must have strength.

La Bruja's games with the other foals in the herd
strengthened the muscles of her legs, taught her to
twist and turn with alacrity, how to defend herself
from unexpected attacks—playful though they might
be—and La Bruja became the most energetic foal in the
herd, for she never tired of running and playing and
teasing. Even the hot summer sun seemed to affect her
but little and when the others were often listless,
flopped out in the grass, La Bruja would be circling
round them on her gawky legs, nibbling and lightly
kicking, trying to coax them to play.

The herd to which La Bruja belonged was small in
comparison with many another wild herd in those days,
which sometimes numbered sixty or seventy or even a
hundred horses. There were only twenty-one animals
in La Bruja's herd, including eight foals, but the stallion who led them was satisfied.

He was a young animal, little more than a colt, and
this was his first herd. The eight foals were the first
of his offspring and, excluding La Bruja, all had inherited his good looks. Small but strong-chested, with
wiry legs and solid frame, he pranced proudly about
his little herd, and by his constant watchfulness and
anger against any mare who showed the slightest disobedience he revealed the fact that this was his first
command.

How grandly he arched his neck, the muscles showing thick in the curve; how alert and eager were his
sparkling eyes; how gaily held was his tail as, reveling
in the sheer joy of being strong and young, he galloped
across the flat grassland, circling his mares at wide distances but never for one moment removing his gaze

from them. His khaki coloring was broken only by a
clear white star on his forehead, black mane, tail and
fetlocks. He was proud in his youth and strength, and
his strength was in the number of his mares.

His sons and daughters feared him, all except La
Bruja. The ungainly, half-breed filly-foal feared nothing. Even as a youngster she was proud, for she inherited this from her sire if nothing else, this and her
love of freedom. She listened to the pounding hoofs
of the restless stallion, watched him as he swooped
around his mares, and while she listened and watched
her own legs would tremble and her heart would beat
faster, for even as a foal she loved to run.

One day the watching and listening became too
much for her. Recklessly, she flung herself after the
racing stallion and followed far behind him, not kicking and bucking as did he, but loping with all the
vigor her young body possessed. The mares and colts
watched in sudden astonishment, for they knew the
bad temper of their master when crossed in his commands.

The mother of La Bruja whinnied shrilly, demand-
ing the filly's return, but the blood was in her head
and her heart expanded thrillingly. La Bruja ignored
her mother. This was everything.

The stallion became aware of his tiny follower and
he whirled suddenly to face her. La Bruja, astonished,
halted and she trembled, not from awe or fear but
from exertion. Ugly head held high, she awaited the
stallion's approach, unmoving while he stalked about
her, sniffing and curious, not angry.

In general the stallion ignored his sons and daughters. They were too young yet either to interest or antagonize him, but La Bruja beheld him fearlessly and he was curious. He touched the panting body with his soft muzzle and it was a gentle touch. Then he turned sharply away again and dashed toward his herd, careering through the startled mares, scattering them deliberately so that he might round them up again.

La Bruja followed him and ever after that she was his shadow. Neither colt nor filly could keep apace with him except La Bruja and only this one ugly offspring would he tolerate.

How superior became La Bruja, indulging in the patronage of her sire. The older colts she battled with, the younger she ignored, and always she had the advantage, for when she chose to flee from their combined rage none could overtake her. How independent she became, going only to her mother for milk and nightly shelter. If she should fall asleep during the daylight hours, made sleepy by a full, contented belly, the faithful mother kept watchful guard over her and stood so that her shadow should fall across La Bruja and keep her from the sun.

La Bruja was unaware of the goodness of her mother. To the filly, the mother was a background to her life, like the sun in the daytime sky, the moon and stars at night, the grass and the wind and the earth. Her mother was food and shelter, nothing more, but when La Bruja lost her mother her life was changed and the joy was gone from living.

Chapter 2

PAMPERO

I

As La Bruja grew, the rising and setting of the sun and moon marking off the days and weeks, the mantle of summer descended upon the land in which the herd dwelt.

The greenness of spring slowly passed away. The grass withered in the heat and became yellowy brown. The giant thistles died, their stalks becoming hollow, their roots turning to dust, but so thickly did they grow together that even rootless they stood, leaning one against the other, supporting each other in huge, rust-brown clumps. They could not fall and they hemmed in the wild horses like high barricades, so that even the docile mares became impatient while the high-spirited stallion was almost savage with rage and La Bruja shared his anger.

For days, weeks and months the thistles stood. At times the summer heat would flare into crackling flames among the tinder-dry stalks and for many miles a vast line of fire would burn, destroying the burrowing vizcachas and other rodents as it crept across the pampa, halting only at a river, stopped only by a storm, or stamped out by the men on the pampa, the gauchos.

Fortunately, fire was not a peril that La Bruja's herd needed to face. The quencher of fire, the destroyer of

thistles and the killer of La Bruja's mother was the
summer storm which came when La Bruja had known
only four months of life.

The storm, pampero it is called by man, came from
the southwest. The afternoon had been long, hot and
still. The north wind, which had been blowing for days
with breath like the heat of a furnace, suddenly
stopped and there was a pregnant silence over the
pampa as the mares and younglings sprawled upon the
ground, exhausted by the heat and breathless atmos-
phere.

A gloom seemed suddenly to possess the sky, a gloom
not cast by any cloud. Even as the horses noticed it
the gloom became a mountain of blackness, clouds of
yellow dust intermingled with it and flocks of terrified
birds, flying madly before the encroaching evil, swept
above the horses and caused them to spring to all fours,
uttering cries of alarm.

Gulls circled and dived and mewed like injured
puma kittens; golden plover thronged with them and
cried their warning too; and a host of monster dragon-
flies clouded the sky when they had gone.

The mares, colts and fillies crushed together in a
frightened bunch and the stallion stayed beside them,
for even he was powerless against the furies of the sky.

Hardly had the birds and insects passed when the
first huge drops of rain began to fall. They came as
liquid mud, falling from a sky choked with windswept
dust. The horses clung to one another as sudden
lightning flashed through the blackness of the clouds
with terrifying thunder close in succession. Torrents of
rain feel upon the cringing horses. They shrieked in

fear at the vivid flashes of light and reared as the thunder rocketed in their sensitive ears.

The stallion was made savage by the tempest. The uproar of sound and sudden light among the darkness filled him with a sense of danger and he watched over his mares with unhesitant cruelty, fearing for them in this fury of the heavens. Any mare that broke away, dashing madly she knew not whither, the stallion raced after to turn her back, kicking, biting, fearful in his rage, and the mares obeyed him, fearing his fury as much as they feared that of the storm.

The first blackness passed away and the air was made white with fleetly falling hailstones; giant hailstones as large as eggs, flat and jagged, and they fell with fury until the pampa was made white with them.

The horses screamed and panicked. Even the stallion could not control them. Beaten by wind and rain and stones of ice they fled hither and thither, but there was no shelter from the tempest and one of them was blinded by the lightning which struck her as she reared in terror.

The storm passed over. The hail ceased, the thunder was silent and by nightfall the pampa was calm again and cool. The horses slept where they stood and when dawn came brilliant sunshine spread over the land and the air was fresh, without a vapor.

But what destruction had the pampero wrought? Now the pampa was a vista of flatness unto the horizon for every thistle had been crushed to the ground and swept away by the violent wind. Plover lay in scores upon the earth, life crushed from them before they could escape, and many more fluttered with broken wings or limped among their dead companions because they could not fly at all.

Tiny deer which frequented the pampa lay dead also, but among the horses the mother of La Bruja had been the only fatality. Struck between the eyes by a heavy hailstone, she fell instantly dead and from that moment the life of her foal was altered.

All the mares wandered about stupefied, suffering from cuts and bruises, some limping as they dragged an injured leg, and they were so much hurt that for days they seemed only semiconscious. Even the proud stallion drooped his head and had no desire to stretch his sturdy legs.

This period of depression passed, for, now that the storm had spent itself, the weather was beautiful and the sun shone without too great a heat and the breezes were cool instead of sultry.

The thistles were gone and the stallion could race again, for there was nothing to impede his stride. But the fleet shadow of La Bruja no longer dogged his path, for now she was an orphan and none to tend her needs. All her energy must be preserved for the unfairly balanced struggled for survival and there was no time for rejoicing and playing and running. She must fight all day and dart from hating hoofs, for there was no mother to defend or feed her.

La Bruja's hope for survival lay with her persistent, strong-willed nature and her speed. To get her daily food she had to steal from every nursing mare, pushing aside the rightful colt or filly to snatch at the udder herself. One or two swallows were all she would gain before being roughly thrust aside, and in this manner she went from mare to mare, tolerated by none, attacked by all, even by the other younglings whose milk she stole.

She had no other manner of living and the favor of the stallion was useless to her. He could not feed her and his mares refused. They kicked her, they bit her, they chased her away and only her fleetness saved her from many a cruel attack. But hunger possessed her and pain became of secondary importance. For the milk of life she would endure much, and spent all the daylight hours robbing the mares as they grazed, regardless of how they punished her.

La Bruja became an outcast among them, a hindrance, and they did not want her. But she ignored their plainly expressed dislike of her because she needed them.

II

It was in the early days that La Bruja missed her mother most; the days before she learned to fend for herself, before she learned to accept the kicks and bites that were the price of a mouthful of milk; the days before she learned to sleep alone.

When the storm had passed La Bruja searched vainly for her mother among the downcast mares, sniffing at them in order to know them and turning away lost when each time she did not find her mother. Then, bewildered, hungry and lonely, she found her mother's body lying among the broken thistles, already stiffening into the rigor of death. She drew back, nose wrinkling

with disgust, ears flattened with fear, for although this
was her mother it was not her mother, and she turned
away from the cold carcass, somehow understanding
that she need search no further for the mother she had
lost.

What was she to do, a four-month suckling without
its dam?

She saw the other colts clinging close to protective
mother flanks; she saw them suckling with stamping
hoofs and flicking tails; she watched them sink repleted
into the grass, ready to sleep away their fullness in
readiness to gorge again. She watched them standing
afar off, for there was none to call her close with a
gentle nicker or a toss of the head.

She was aware of great hunger as she watched and
when all had fed and fallen asleep only then did she
attempt to approach the several mothers, searching for
a little kindness, a tiny neigh of welcome. There was
neither. They treated her tentative advances roughly,
thrusting her aside without mercy. They had milk
enough for one colt only and nature was hard on the
motherless.

All that day La Bruja starved. She slept awhile, lying
at a distance from the herd, and the warm sun melting
over her back gave her comfort, she to whom all maternal comfort was now denied.

La Bruja felt loneliness as well as hunger. She had
never slept alone before. There had always been her
dam beside her, guarding her while she slumbered.
Now she had no patient watcher, one to see that no
puma stole upon her while she slept, that no colt or
jealous mare would suddenly attack her.

With the coming of the second dawn after the storm
La Bruja was desperate in her hunger and so this day
she began to rob the mares of the milk they would not
give her, regardless of the cost. She ended the day
battered and bruised, but her craving hunger had been
almost satisfied and she could sleep without pain, half
contented.

So passed each succeeding day and La Bruja thrived,
thin and ragged ever but lively still. The loss of her
mother became no longer a grievance with her, but for
many a week she felt her absence. She had been hardly
aware of her mother while she lived, but now that she
was gone La Bruja was greatly aware of her loss.

She was friendless and alone, unprotected from the
daily fears and bumps in every childhood, animal or
human. She did not miss her mother with an aching
heart but only with a knowledge that she lacked something she needed. She had no comfort or anchorage
and life was hard because of it. Otherwise in her slight
memory her mother no longer existed.

The daily disturbance among the mares roused by La
Bruja was not unnoticed by the stallion and he grew
resentful toward the gangling filly who constantly scattered his herd. His former tolerance for her was forgotten and he himself turned upon her and drove her
away. La Bruja knew no fear of the stallion and his
punishments were no harder to bear than those of the
mares. She side-jumped and sometimes fled, but as
soon as the moment was opportune she cautiously returned again, driven by hunger and even by defiance.

La Bruja no longer galloped behind her sire, nor did

she even watch him. She cared for nothing now, intent only upon survival, and, while necessity forced her, she robbed the mares of their jealously guarded milk, robbed them until she no longer needed it.

This day came gradually, week by week, as she grew. She began to notice the grass beneath her hoofs and when she was nearing six months of age it attracted her. She nuzzled it with her pink nostrils, snorting as its coolness tickled her; she gingerly tested it with her tongue and slowly she took her first bites of it, finding it strange but somehow satisfying.

Soon she was daily cropping the grass, finding patches of sweet clover, a delicacy of which she never tired. Milk became of secondary importance to her and it was not long before she surrendered it completely and lived by grass alone.

When she became this much independent she ignored the mares completely. Her bruises faded, her split skin healed and a glow began to come to her coat which before had been rough and dull.

La Bruja grazed away from her herd. She chose to be alone, scorning the others as any outcast scorns those who turn him away, but an inherent need for safety kept her within sight of the mares. Still she needed their protection, for alone she was well-nigh helpless against her foes, especially at so young an age.

The stallion watched over her from a distance. He sometimes circled round her and drove her toward the herd, but she resisted all his efforts to keep her among his mares, and after a while he let her alone, seeing that she did not intend to stray.

She was a satellite, outcast like Hagar, but she was a female and belonged to the stallion. He would make certain that she did not wander. As he would drive away the colts when they reached maturity, so would he cling to the fillies and keep them near him.

Chapter 3

SECOND SPRING

I

La Bruja, dwelling almost alone, learned much about the pampa on which she lived. Now that grass and clover were her diet, she no longer felt hunger and, after grazing, she found time enough to explore and discover and play.

She learned that there was other life apart from that of the herd. There were timid deer, dwelling in groups that kept well apart from the horses. Their smell was strong and unpleasant and La Bruja snorted her disgust with wrinkled nostrils whenever she came upon them.

There were guanacos, the llama of the pampa, smaller than their mountain brothers but much the same in every other respect. Their necks were tall, their ears were long and their heads were haughtily stupid. La Bruja found them curious and she learned that they were not to be feared.

There were the huge rheas, the flightless giant bird that lived among the guanacos and sometimes among the horses. They were powerful and fleet, vicious when aroused, and La Bruja kept well clear of them, for they often startled her.

Below her hoofs teemed much more life, for there were rodents of many kinds burrowing beneath the pampa grass. Nocturnal creatures, La Bruja saw little of them, but the vizcachas built complicated labyrinths below the ground and left evidence of this in the huge piles of sun-baked earth which were scattered generously about the pampa, conspicuous at any distance. When La Bruja was small they were big enough to make the jumping of them an exciting game, but, as she grew, they seemed to shrink and, after a while, no longer interested her.

While she daily discovered new things, La Bruja grew and signs of babyhood fell away. The brushy tail vanished, and dark, slender hair grew down to her hocks. The tufts along her neck became a proper mane and forelock, falling freely about her but not adding much to her general appearance.

She grew much. Her long legs became even longer, her long body too. There was alertness in her luminous eyes, but defiance too which detracted from their beauty. Her liver coloring did not change, except to darken, and there was not even a white marking on her forehead to bring some small attraction to the roman nose and gaunt, plain features. She was taller than any of her sisters or brothers and she was fast overtaking her sire, a fourteen-hand pony, tall enough for his breed.

Winter came to the pampa and with it came coldness and rain and days without sun to which La Bruja was not accustomed. The summer birds fled and the stallion considered it time to drive his herd northward to a warmer clime.

They traveled slowly, grazing in a leisurely fashion as they went, many of the mares in foal again but with a

La Bruja became an outcast among them.

youngster still running at their heels. The grass was
ever abundant and as they journeyed northward they
came to warmer winds and more sunshine.

La Bruja traveled behind, with them but not of them.
She had accepted her lonely life unquestioningly and
was contented enough to live as she did. She felt no
need of comradeship, for, after being denied it so long,
the desire in her had faded and she was glad to graze
alone.

All winter through they turned their heads northward, but when the first signs of spring were coming to
the pampa the stallion changed direction and back they
trekked to their own country, leaving rocky scrubland
and distant forests behind them.

Fresh green grass was springing up. The patches of
weeds which grew thick and tall in the summer months
fell away to nothing during the winter and the grass
could find its way. The rhythm of spring was in the
air. Swallows returned to their nests, flying above the
heads of the horses as they journeyed swiftly to their
homes. The mornings were misty and fresh, damp and
clean. Lapwings cried and drummed their wings; pipits
soared high and poured out songs of spring as they
floated slowly earthward. The mares gave birth to the
new year's foals and the yearlings could not understand
why their mothers did not heed them.

The thistles came again and La Bruja found their
huge, rhubarb-like leaves good to eat. The stems were
sweet and La Bruja ignored the grass to take her fill of
this new tasting plant which she had been too young
to discover before. She grew fat on these leaves and

firm flesh covered her ribs so that they were no longer conspicuous.

As time passed the thistles grew hard and dry and were not fit to eat. Their flowers broke open in a white mass, shedding scores of silvery seeds which floated aloft in the breeze. Then the whole sky seemed to be a myriad of silvery balls, floating hither and thither, and the horses tossed their heads and sneezed, but eagerly snaffled up the fallen seeds which abundantly covered the ground. They flourished on them because they were good.

The days were spent in idleness and feasting. La Bruja watched and felt all the signs of her second spring and her spirit grew high and glad as such flowing life came to the pampa anew.

She kicked and bucked and dashed about, stretching her long, slender legs into a wild gallop, and the mares watched her with mild surprise, having not the energy for such useless play. With new life in the herd they were fully occupied caring for their foals and they were loath to do more than eat and doze and guard their younglings.

II

When La Bruja was a yearling the stallion claimed her and brought her into the herd, keeping her there with many bites and kicks, for she was unwilling to stay among the mares, she who was accustomed to dwelling alone.

The stallion was pugnacious now, more than he had ever been, and the slightest disobedience by any mare he would not tolerate. In this time of marauding stallions he was jealous for each member of his herd and would permit no straying for fear that one of his mares would be stolen away.

He first attacked the yearling colts, his three handsome sons that had hardly recovered from the separation from their dams. He drove them away with squeals of rage, eyes flashing, hoofs rearing over them, ready to strike if they did not obey his commands. Bewildered and greatly frightened, they scattered across the pampa and the stallion chased each one in turn, biting them in the rump in order to let them know his power.

The three colts stayed together. They did not entirely desert the herd for some time, still full of longing for their mothers and companions, unable to understand the jealousy of their sire. After a while they slowly wandered away, became independent and proud, becoming stallions themselves one day and treating their sons as they had been treated by their father.

The stallion had his battles too. Even though his herd was small it was coveted, while he in his turn desired the mares of others. His biggest battle was with a small, skewbald stallion, twice his age and with twice his number of mares.

They fought hard and savagely, rearing to their hind legs and using their forehoofs to inflict damage, screaming all the while. Neither could gain the advantage and by mutual consent they fell away from each other, returning to their respective herds, scarred and weary. La Bruja's sire had the left ear completely torn away, while the other went from that day blinded in one eye by a blow from the other's hoof.

Lesser battles gained the stallion eight more mares and fewer scars. Some of his youthful handsomeness was gone, but great was his glory when he surveyed his growing herd. When the time of fighting passed he settled down to guard his mares from their daily and often non-existent enemies, his wounds healing, his pride increasing.

He allowed La Bruja to stray again, for he had no fear for her now. There was no stallion to molest and steal her. She had a growing foal within her and was safe.

La Bruja was unaware of the foal. She was glad to find herself free from the stallion's domination, able to dwell in her solitary fashion, for even now the mares resented her, a stranger in their midst, and they treated her no better than before. The eight new mares came in for some hazing too, but they gradually settled down among their new companions, a thing that independent La Bruja could not do. She longed for her solitude while she was with them and when spring had passed and summer came she took advantage of her sire's relaxed vigilance and separated herself from them again.

The months of summer dried the grass, which wilted yellow and pale beneath the blazing sun. When the thistles and their seeds had withered the mares' new fatness melted away. This summer there were not so many thistles and the stallion galloped proudly around his larger herd which now contained twenty-five mares and fifteen colts. ·

As time passed, La Bruja felt not so inclined to gallop. She was becoming aware of the growing foal, and, though not understanding its meaning, a slothful spirit overtook her, she who had delighted in stretching her lanky legs into a race with the wind. A feeling of contentment filled her, so that she desired only to eat and doze like the others.

The burning sun dried up the lakes, and the golden plover, which had come in hundreds from colder climes, fled the pampa in search of water. The horses traveled from district to district, searching the same, and there were many days when their thirsts remained unslaked for it did not rain. The mud at the lakesides was cracked and dry and the mares surveyed each parched lagoon with dismal eyes. Then came a time of fierce storms which drove away the scorching heat and filled the lakes again. But no storm this year compared in severity with that which killed La Bruja's mother.

Autumn came, bringing with it new grass, damp with luscious sap. The mares ate ravenously and all their days were spent thus, eating and teaching their youngsters to eat. Flocks of squalling, hurrying birds, sweeping northward, warned the mares of the coldness to come and the stallion once again looked to the north, heeding their warning, for the birds were true messengers often.

Winter came and passed away and La Bruja's third spring was nearing, the time when she would bring forth a colt or filly, as had her mother before her. She was uglier than ever in her hugeness and it did not seem that her ugliness would ever fall away, for it increased with every year. Her thinness was her nature and she could never be fat like the Criollos because of the blood of her grandsire, the tall and slender thoroughbred who passed on his thinness but not his beauty.

La Bruja instinctively began to learn about the life within her and somehow she knew that within a short time she must find a safe and secret place. It was not enough to stay at her present distance from the herd, for might they not search her out in curiosity and then, in jealousy, kill what she had nurtured for so long? No chances must be taken, this she knew, and she sought out a thicket of tall grass as she grazed, examining it with care.

It was soft and warm and sheltered. As the herd wandered along they would within a day or two be at some distance from the place La Bruja chose, near enough to return to if danger threatened but far enough to be at peace and fearless.

La Bruja chose wisely. She had not done this thing before, but instinct came to her aid without her knowing and she did that which instinct commanded as if it were her own desire. She lingered near her chosen place and the other mares went on. The stallion allowed her to linger this much more than usual, for he knew that after two or three days alone she would return to the herd, foal at heels, and his herd would be increased again.

Chapter 4

THE MOTHER

I

La Bruja's time had come. She lay in the thicket and was glad to be alone. Her ears were alert, straining for any sound unusual, and she watched the birds. By their actions she would know if all were well. They would sing and swoop and play in the air, but if danger came they would screech and flap their wings and vanish. Now they played and their joyful twitterings and song were a soothing background to La Bruja's patient suffering.

The early days of spring were short and the sun soon deserted the sky, leaving the pampa to the pleasure of the moon and its sparkling companions. La Bruja was restless and a little afraid. There were few nights that she had seen and none that she had experienced so completely alone.

She rose and stretched and grazed a little. She trembled at strange rustlings and the sobs of a crazy widow bird, and she returned to the thicket, which was warm still from the heat of her body.

The foal came and it was in darkness that La Bruja began her first duties of motherhood. The moon had suddenly vanished behind a mass of cloud and it was by smell alone that La Bruja found her youngling and cleaned it. She heard its tiny breathing and felt its

warmth and she was flooded with rich desires to love
and tend the little creature dropped in the thicket.

With such eagerness she licked it clean; with such
contentment she listened to its first struggles to rise,
its wavering bleats of determination, for in the darkness she could make out nothing of the foal. The moon
had failed her when she needed it most.

The clouds floated on and the moon returned once
more in all its glory. La Bruja saw by its powerful light
the foal she had only heard and felt. It was already
rocking unsteadily on its tiny hoofs and the spindle
legs trembled at the strength with which they were
suddenly empowered.

A filly-foal it was and in appearance she was all that
a Criollo foal should be, with none of La Bruja's ugliness
or strangeness and all of her sire's good looks. She was
tiny, of color a rusty yellow which was to become a
mellowed bronze with age. Time was to bring her to
captivity and the tiny creature, now filling La Bruja's
heart with love and joy, was to become the joy of a
gaucho poet, a payador, who called her Thamár, for
she was as beautiful as the daughter of a king.

As La Bruja had done in her time, the filly-foal
Thamár learned hastily the use of her legs, as must
learn all young creatures born on the plain where there
are no places to hide in safety. Hunger, too, she felt
and La Bruja was aware of the eagerly searching, soft
little mouth with a contentment she had never known
before.

Here was company at last, something of her own
which would never deny her or drive her away, something which needed her as once she had needed her

dam. With gladness she gave herself to Thamár and stood in patience while she sucked.

Dawn came in a glow of pink and gold. Below the color of the sky a thick, white mist wreathed among the grass and slowly dispersed, leaving a fresh dampness over the earth and a sparkling dew which quenched the thirsty mother as she ate, coming eagerly from the thicket with the foal dancing excitedly beside her. The mist clung ghost-like to their warm bodies and when La Bruja plunged her head to eat there was no sign of it. Her legs, too, were invisible and there was little to see of Thamár, shivering beside her.

Unlike her mother, La Bruja felt no desire to return to the herd and the protection of the stallion. What was there to call to she who had always dwelt in loneliness? She had no memories of friendliness and company and never had the pampa given her cause to fear. Why needed she protection? What needed she to fear?

The stallion had kept her in unwilling bondage and now she was free. With Thamár at her side she had all the company she needed and she was unwilling to take her filly to the herd. There would be no welcoming neighs, no friendly touch of noses, only iron hoofs and cruel teeth.

Hardly aware of her intentions, La Bruja drifted away from the herd. She knew full well in which direction it was and she turned her head the other way. As the hours passed and the sun grew warmer, La Bruja became resolved in her decision.

The filly took her fill of milk and basked beside her. La Bruja stood so that her shadow should fall across the little creature, for there were no trees on the

pampa to give respite from the sun. While Thamár slept,
La Bruja stood guard and in everything she did she
was contented. No danger threatened, the birds all sang
and played and nothing could persuade La Bruja to
return to her rightful place. She feared nothing, for
her legs were swift and her heart was strong.

When the filly woke, refreshed and lively, La Bruja
watched her play. She chased the multicolored butterflies, she reared up to snatch at the plover as she
caught their shadows overhead, and she grabbed her
mother's swishing tail, anxious to prove her strength
and to use her so newly discovered legs. Then La
Bruja put a stop to play, for, now that she had made
a decision, she was anxious to put more distance between herself and the herd and also from the place
wherein Thamár had been born.

She set off at a trot and Thamár was glad to follow
her, thinking this some new game that her mother
played. She raced ahead and turned to watch her
slower mother, but very soon tiredness and hunger
overcame her so that La Bruja had to halt and allow
the foal to feed.

In this manner the hours passed by and soon darkness came upon the land again. The foal slept and La
Bruja kept watch over her. Her restless spirit was somewhat quieted, for by this time she and Thamár were
at some distance from the herd. From now on it was
certain that they would dwell alone.

II

La Bruja's decision to dwell alone with Thamár was
not a wise one. She who had known only three springs

could be hardly aware of the dangers that waited on a lonely mare. The lion which would cautiously withdraw from a herd guarded by a watchful stallion had no fear of stragglers or strays.

Then there was man—that all powerful, deadly creature whom La Bruja had never seen. How could she even know that man was as great an enemy as the puma and more clever? Man made slaves of horses and these horses betrayed their own kind. La Bruja feared no horse and she could not know that the creature he carried on his back was dangerous.

These two dangers were the greatest, for, apart from puma and man, there were few creatures to harm her.

La Bruja had no fears. In her ignorance she grazed and guarded her youngling with only instinct to make her sniff the air and keep her ears alert. For what was she listening? Would she recognize the scent of danger when it came?

Not only because of ignorance was La Bruja unafraid. She was aware of her great speed and she had already learned that speed was the greatest asset in life. She could excel her own sire in the race and for this knowledge of her ability she was unafraid.

La Bruja rarely galloped these days. Thamár could not keep apace with her if she did and La Bruja refused to be separated from her foal by more than a length or two. She guarded the filly with great zeal, for her heart cleaved to this little creature which was her own, and Thamár was La Bruja's life.

With joy she watched her youngling play, showing her games at times, for she was still a filly herself and young enough to play. When Thamár grew weary La

Bruja would draw the foal to her with tenderness, gently nibbling her neck and caressing her by brushing her head against the filly's body. She was all that any foal could desire and in the shadow of her mother's care Thamár grew strong and bold and beautiful, the latter attribute being even more striking in contrast to La Bruja's ugliness.

The daily life of mother and foal was uneventful. They passed each hour by eating, playing, sleeping and partaking in the general activity of the pampa. They saw no other horses and for this La Bruja was glad. She wanted no company but that of Thamár and she was rich in contentment, for life now treated her well. But, by the very order of things, La Bruja's folly in choosing to live this solitary life was made apparent, for it is ordained that her kind must live together in order to be safe.

The summer days had passed and the first autumn chills were in the air. Grass was shooting up again, succulent and green, and La Bruja's pleasure and greed for the new season's offerings perhaps made her less wary than usual. Also, she had lived unmolested for half a year and confidence bred contempt.

Her first awareness of danger came too late. The young, fawn puma crouching among the grass and tangled clumps of withered weeds sprang suddenly upon her, and La Bruja, in surprise, could only scream out shrilly her fear and pain as claws dug deeply into her withers and teeth gnawed at her neck.

Then instinct forced itself uppermost in the midst of her confusion. With a mighty jerk of the head, she reared high and flung the puma from her. As he flopped

to the ground La Bruja fled and her heart beat heavily
as her hoofs pounded across the pampa, fear subsid-
ing a little as she recognized her power in speed. She
gave not even a backward glance to tarry her, but
dashed away, forgetting the pain, forgetting everything in her dread of the puma.

A terrified cry smote upon her ears, a cry she knew
at once for that of Thamár. She had forgotten her foal
in her moment of danger and the sudden realization of
this halted instantly her crazed career. She swirled
about and saw the lithe and hungry puma bounding
after her youngling, almost within reach but never
quite. Thamár was not so swift as her dam, but fear
lent speed to her and her legs galloped swiftly while
her heart was frozen.

The mother came to her rescue. Moments earlier, the
puma had terrified her, but now her heart was filled
with scorching rage against the creature that threatened Thamár. Speed had carried her to safety, now it
brought her back into danger with the strength and
fury of a whirlwind.

She charged upon the puma, mouth open, teeth
bared, eyes rolling white, screaming with wild rage as
she attacked him. The puma gave up his second prey
and turned to face his attacker with snarls and hisses,
not swift enough to flee. He crouched to the ground
and clawed at her and La Bruja's heavy hoofs came
slicing down upon him. He dodged them and sprang
at her before she could strike again and now he was
upon her back, clinging like moss to a stone, and La
Bruja could not shake him off.

Undaunted, she flung herself upon the ground and

rolled over and the puma jumped aside to save himself. He was quicker than La Bruja and before she
could spring to her feet he had grabbed her neck,
sure that this time he was the victor. But he had not
reckoned with a mother's love and La Bruja somehow
managed to strike him as he clung to her, dashing
him to the ground.

Dazed, he could not escape her now. She crashed her
hoofs upon him again and again, white froth foaming
from her jaws, blood streaming from her in many
places. The puma hissed and cried and howled, but
La Bruja, with the cry of her own youngling still in
her ears, had no mercy for her defeated foe.

She crushed his soft body completely, even when he
was dead. Not until the flesh was pulp and the bones
all cracked did La Bruja cease her stamping and when
she stopped her rage had cooled and she had forgotten
Thamár's terrified cry. Then she became aware of soreness and exhaustion and also a violent thirst. She was
trembling, every limb aching with exertion, but her
first concern was Thamár.

She nickered softly to the frightened foal and drew
her gently to her, searching all parts of the slender
body in order to discover if it had received any injury.
Thamár was whole, however, and La Bruja's heart was
eased.

Together they trotted to the nearest watering place
and by nightfall the fear of the afternoon had completely faded, although La Bruja was never to forget
the experience and for ever afterward held a deep hatred for the pampa lion.

Chapter 5

THE ROUNDUP

La Bruja's wounds healed. Several scars marked her neck and withers ever afterward to tell of the battle she had fought with the puma, but no injury was deep enough to cause any permanent damage or impede her swiftness. The scars made her more ugly, but of this La Bruja was unaware. Thamár was unharmed and this was her only interest. She learned to guard herself and her youngling with more care and never again was she taken unaware by a puma.

That autumn La Bruja also caught her first sight of man. She was grazing unconcernedly, Thamár not far distant sniffing at the clover and taking her first taste of it, when she suddenly heard fast hoofbeats a short distance from her. She looked up startled, staring with pricked ears and watchful eyes at the horse whose hoofs she heard, and saw a strange creature upon his back.

The horse was galloping madly, not toward La Bruja but away, and therefore she did not stir from where she stood, curiosity overwhelming any slight instinct of danger. The horse she understood well enough, but what was it he carried astride him? Some living creature assuredly, for it made sounds and moved.

The gaucho wore a poncho round his shoulders and

this streamed out behind him as he raced against the
wind, adding to the strangeness of his figure. Perhaps
he did not see La Bruja, or perhaps he saw only her
ugliness and regarded her as worthless. Certainly he
did not turn toward her but left her unmolested, where
she stood to wonder at this oddity which she had
never seen before.

The horse and rider passed by, but, because the
pampa is flat, La Bruja was able to watch them for
some time, growing smaller in size, fainter in sound,
until eventually she lost interest and returned to grazing.

This was La Bruja's first sight of man and it was
not alarming. Like a bird that sweeps overhead, so
came and went the gaucho and his horse, pausing for
nothing. La Bruja soon forgot him and when man came
again she was unafraid, having no reason to fear.

La Bruja should have feared the second time, which
shortly followed the first. A great roundup of wild
horses had been arranged by the gauchos. They wanted
the horses for two reasons. The first reason was in order
to sell the hides and grease to traders, who sent them
across the seas to other lands; the second was to keep
and break any of the ponies too worthy of such an end.

They had planned the roundup with care. They
built a huge stockade and they sent out riders to learn
where the horses dwelt, so that they should know how
great a drive they would need to make in order to
capture them all. The first rider La Bruja saw was such
a man and he returned with reports of two large herds
and a few odd strays within the district he had
searched. Other reports were similar and the gauchos

concluded with their rough arithmetic that, with luck, they should within a week ensnare perhaps two hundred horses.

The gaucho of those times had more Indian than European blood in his veins. His skin was dark, his eyes and hair black, his body supple and strong. He had inherited the primitive skills of the Indian, the pride of the Spaniard, and combined the two with the natural simplicity of the poor, uneducated man. His heart could be callous and cruel, his actions savage, and yet he could be quickly warmed to friendship, was rarely dishonest and believed implicitly in the religion of the Spaniards. The horse of the pampa was his greatest friend and highly esteemed, but, at the same time, often suffered cruelly in his hands.

There were thirty such men to partake in the round-up and six more to guard the stockade and keep it prepared for the first onslaught of trampling, frightened horses. The thirty gauchos planned to ride in V-formation, boleadoras at the ready to cut down any would-be escaper, dogs to help them where needed. They looked forward to the roundup with great excitement. There would be much hard riding, much killing and much fighting with unbroken horses. What more could any gaucho desire?

La Bruja was unaware of the danger which threatened. She grazed unconcernedly throughout the days and there was nothing to bring fear to her. Perhaps if she had known of man and learned to fear him she would have taken warning from the gaucho she saw,

but within a few hours she had not even a memory
of him.

Other horses in that district were a little afraid. Most
of them had had some experience of man, enough to
set them trembling at the occasional sight of one, and
in the last few days they had been aware of much galloping of hoofs and several men, who, though not
touching them, filled them with a sense of foreboding
difficult to shake off. Stallions kept their mares in tight
bunches, allowing no stragglers, so that their attention
need never be diverted from the search for danger.

It was the birds that gave the first warnings. They
swept across the sky in ever-increasing numbers,
screeching down to the horses of what they had seen,
disturbed from their ground nests by the hunters who
advanced slowly but surely across the pampa.

Stallions, mares and youngsters all looked up,
alerted, and they began to follow the birds, uncertainly
at first, not having yet seen the danger, but growing in
confidence as other pampa creatures came in their
wake.

A dozen frightened deer, a herd of loping guanacos,
intermingled with flustered rheas. Now the horses were
certain of danger and from which direction it came.

They spent little time grazing, but eagerly followed
the stallions as they led the way to safety. Eventually,
as the gauchos had carefully planned it, the various
herds met and at first there was bickering among the
mares and fighting among the stallions until they realized their common danger and combined together to
defeat it.

Five separate herds united into one swell of mares,

colts and stallions, keeping their individuality as much as was possible, all journeying unwittingly toward the stockade, thinking, as this was the only way open to them, that it must be the way to freedom.

La Bruja and Thamár came too, mingling unnoticed among the others. La Bruja was reluctant to surrender her solitary state, but she felt safe among so many. There were young colts, not two years old, and several lone stallions, for the gauchos had spread over a wide area in order to draw so many into their trap.

The horses traveled with increasing fear, bewilderment and speed, not knowing from what they fled but given no time to stop and puzzle things out. All they knew was that some mysterious power had forced them together against their will and that the birds gave warning that the power was fearsome, drawing closer each day.

Suddenly the enemy declared itself, on a morning sunny and fresh and seemingly calm. From every direction except in front of them came a wildly screeching, whip flapping, madly galloping gauchos, with baying dogs beside them. The astonished, pertrified herd stared incredulously, whinnying, neighing, stricken with panic.

Of one accord they broke into a mad gallop, blundering into one another before deciding upon a general direction, then fleeing one behind the other blindly, recklessly, wherever the gauchos chose to drive them. When the first panic died many of them realized that a trap awaited them, and sometimes individually, sometimes two or three together, they struggled out of the crush and tried to escape alone in a different direction.

What vain hope was this! Whips and savage dogs
drove them back again or cleverly thrown boleadoras
entwined themselves about their legs and brought them
headlong to the ground.

Not a single horse escaped, not even La Bruja and
Thamár. Those that remained behind on the pampa
were the perhaps fortunate dead, two or three that had
fallen in the general stampede and had life crushed
from them by trampling hoofs that could not swerve in
time.

Apart from these, they swept unknowingly into the
huge stockade, swirling round, crashing into one
another, falling under one another's hoofs as they were
abruptly brought to a standstill by a towering blockade
on every side. The melee was wild, rough and confused
and the gauchos watched with sparkling eyes and
laughter, already picking out their favorites among the
frightened brutes, consigning the rest to death.

After a while the struggling ceased. Exhaustion overcame them and desperation became dejection. With
drooping heads they stood and panted, tongues lolling
from parched mouths, legs weary almost to crumbling.

Thus the gauchos left them, glad to rest themselves,
in no great hurry to begin the slaughter, for there was
plenty of time in the days to come.

Chapter 6

IN THE STOCKADE

I

La Bruja and Thamár stood together in one corner, pressed hard against the strongly built stockade wall by the many trembling, sweating bodies on every side. Like the rest, they were too dejected and overcome with exhaustion to care about captivity and when the glaring sun had vanished and a soothing darkness filled the sky some of La Bruja's fear faded. Nothing more had happened. Her youngling was unharmed and still beside her. There was the dreadful uncertainty of bewilderment, the hatred of captivity, the crush of bodies all about her, but, apart from this, danger did not seem to threaten.

Unaware of man's power, unaware of man's brutality, unaware of his feelingless heart, La Bruja could not fear more than a little, could not grieve for more than the freedom she had lost. It was too soon for her to realize what freedom meant. Except for the last few hours, she had always been free and knew no other existence.

But when the morning came La Bruja learned to fear and hate and grow violent against man, for not until the morning did she begin to comprehend the nature of her captors. Morning brought death to the stockade, a violent, lingering massacre, which nauseated and terrified the horses as they saw their companions die before them.

One by one the mares not considered fit for riding were captured and killed. While the second died the first was skinned and so it went on all morning until the smell of death choked the clean air and the earth was red. Hawks clung to perches on the stockade, eyes greedily surveying the slaughter, flocking to each carcass as it was cast aside, fighting with screeches and flapping wings even though a feast was spread before them.

So the pampa was violated by man and the spirit of each living horse was crushed by the sight, smell and sound of its dying companions.

La Bruja, squashed in the corner behind terrified mares and stallions, inconspicuous in coloring, was somehow overlooked. To her section was designated every animal reprieved, either for its looks or probable capabilities. They were mostly colts and stallions, for mares were commonplace, rarely ridden by gauchos, so that the few mares saved were young and beautiful, not like La Bruja, who should have died.

The slaughter stopped only when darkness came, but darkness could not destroy the smell of death. The living horses stood in terror and utter disgust, hearing the quarrelsome hawks, which slept with bloated bellies about the corral, as they rustled their feathers and sometimes pecked one another.

The night was peaceful, and the pampa outside the stockade, where the horses had dwelt so shortly since, was sweet and calm and quiet. The same moon that looked down upon the young, fresh grass looked down upon the signs of slaughter. It looked down upon the sleeping gauchos and the trembling horses and it was impartial in its gaze upon horror and beauty.

Another day dawned and with the coming of the sun the hawks began again to scavenge among the bodies that remained. Below the fresh, golden sky of morning shadows faded from the pampa and the slaughterers awoke to share the beauty of the sky before they returned to the work they had begun the day before.

To their knowledge they had killed all the horses they wanted to kill. The rest were to be broken to a rider and put to work. The stallions and colts would be gelded, the several mares considered carefully for breeding, and they would either be kept by the gauchos who broke them or sold to anyone interested enough to buy.

So after a day of death came a day of fighting and, as they were skilled and heartless butchers, so were the gauchos skilled and brutal breakers.

The first stallion was chosen and two men on horseback sorted him out from the others. This was no easy task, for when he divined their intentions he dived into the center of the herd, creating chaos among them. The horses milled and raced about and the screeches of delight uttered by the gauchos only increased their fear and confusion. The stallion, a small, handsome red roan, was brought to the ground by cunning lassos and while he struggled to all fours again one of the ropes was whipped about a post in the center of the stockade while that about his hind leg was dragged over his back, pulling the captured hoof from the ground and leaving him helpless with only three legs to stand on.

A saddle of sheepskin was flung across his back and cinched tightly about him, while he fell again, so that his flesh was puckered and squashed. He could not kick that saddle loose, no matter how hard he tried. A leather halter was fixed about his plunging head with a rein attached and, as the ropes were released and the stallion began to fight, a gaucho sprang on his back and the battle was on.

The fight was furious. The stallion had only his strength and rage while the gaucho had skill, cunning and a pair of sharp spurs tied to his naked heels. The stallion reared and tossed, he twisted and bucked, eyes rolling, mouth open, and with every effort he made the gaucho dug in his spurs and yelled like a savage, clinging to the roan as if he were a hair upon his back. The stallion tried to grab one of the legs that kicked and stung him, but as his head came round and his teeth snapped, a heavy slash from the gaucho's whip across his ear halted him, gasping and half stunned.

The gaucho won the battle and the stallion was his, defeated, exhausted, but still beautiful and worth possessing. Now it was the turn of another man and horse and a similar battle commenced.

So it went on all day. Sometimes the gauchos won, sometimes the horses, though the latter was rare, for if one man gave up there was another to take his place. Sometimes neither won, for a proud, freedom-loving stallion would fight till his heart burst rather than submit himself to man. Then there would be another corpse to skin, another feast for the hawks, but no pity or compassion, never that.

La Bruja's sire was among the latter, the handsome

She charged the puma, screaming with wild rage as she attacked.

khaki-colored stallion with the white starred forehead who so loved to race with the wind, for he with all his mares had been ensnared, to survive them but a day, preferring death to slavery.

Of all his herd only La Bruja remained, she and the foal which he had sired, and sooner or later her fate, too, must be decided. The colts and mares were broken one by one until only a few remained to be dealt with on the following day. Among them was La Bruja.

II

The few horses that remained alive and unbroken in the corral to mope another long night through had been saved for sport on the following day. Now that the work was more or less completed, the gauchos had decided upon a fiesta to satisfy their appetite for fun and laughter. Those who had womenfolk nearby rode in haste to fetch them from their tiny, windowless homes on the pampa, dressed in all their finery; and a payador chanced to pass that way, his guitar slung across his shoulders, and he was begged to stay the night beside their fires and entertain them on the morrow.

There were but four horses unbroken in the stockade, excluding Thamár, and these four were ravenous with hunger and half crazed with thirst, for none had thought to feed and water them. The grass had been crushed beneath so many hoofs and that which remained was rusty with dried blood, so that the horses could find no desire in all their hunger to eat it. Thamár, the only youngster, felt not the discomfort of her

mother or the other three, for, though she had cropped
grass for several weeks, the sweet milk of her dam was
still her staple diet and this satisfied both hunger and
thirst. La Bruja's lean flanks grew leaner and there was
less milk for Thamár, as this was her third night in the
stockade and she had not tasted even a mouthful of
grass or water in all the days between.

Hunger made her savage. The smell of death had
brought fear to her and fear became violent hatred
against those who had wrought the slaughter all about
her. She knew that her time must come to face her
captors and her heart swelled with savage intentions as
she waited.

With so few horses in the large stockade, the gauchos could no longer overlook La Bruja and they saw
her with astonishment. She was so ugly, so colorless,
that some mistake must have been made. Surely no
gaucho had claimed her. Then they saw her foal, the
beautiful, almost golden-coated filly, with black points
like her sire, and each man spoke in admiration of her,
for even at that young age there was no doubt that
she was beautiful.

La Bruja, for Thamár's sake, was reprieved again, so
the mother and daughter spent their last night in the
corral together, the last night that they were ever
more to share.

With the dawning of the following day the gauchos
killed two long-horned cows and a sheep and there
were more moans of death to frighten the horses as
they fell. Hastily skinned and prepared, they were
slowly roasted over beds of burning dung and from the

early hours the savor of sweet melting fat and brown-
ing flesh filled the air. Dogs yelped and whined and
hopefully watched the several carcasses, jaws slavering
with hunger. The wild horses grew restless at this new,
strange smell, for they had an instinctive fear of fire,
but no one noticed them.

The payador seated himself on the skull of a horse
and surveyed the scene in solitude, shaded from the
strength of the morning sun by his faithful mount, an
old, bay gelding who stood behind him with drooping
head and twitching ears. The dark eyes of the payador
lacked the wildness of the gauchos', his face was kindly
and full of understanding. The hair which flowed to
his shoulders was hidden behind a handkerchief tied
about his head beneath his tall sombrero, and his long
gray beard and wrinkled skin gave him the appearance
of a sage.

The payador was something of a sage, for he had
lived long and had been made wise by the things he
had seen, heard and read. This man could read and
the stories he read he told to the gauchos in song and
verse, often inspired to the use of beautiful words
which his listeners, for all their ignorance, appreciated
and understood. In his words was the song of the
pampa; the sounds of spring and winter; birth and
death; and all these things the gauchos knew.

The payador was respected and well loved by all
who knew him, for he was gentle and kind, yet unobtrusively forceful. He told stories of the birds, he
put words into the mouths of animals with understanding and yet with amusement. He could make the gauchos laugh, he could make them sit in silent thought,

for the payador wielded great power with his words and the accompanying guitar.

While the gauchos prepared for the fiesta and worked in their several ways, some idling and chatting with the womenfolk, others loading the last of the half-dried skins into the huge ox-drawn wagons stationed near the stockade, still more guarding the roasts, the payador thought of the stories he would tell them. As well as old favorites they would expect something new and the payador thought of the horses which had died in the corral. He made up a verse about them and plucked the strings of his guitar as words came into his head, for his mind and fingers worked as one.

The gauchos, hearing him, gathered about him and begged to be told of what he thought. The tune was sad, the strings hummed with mournful vibrations, and the payador waited until he had drawn a crowd before he began, conditioning them for the sadness of his song by the hollow sobs of the guitar which throbbed its message to all of them.

The gauchos fell silent and nearby horses turned with pricked ears to listen also. The payador began his song and in his ancient voice was all his widsom, all his understanding, all his remembrance of sorrow and pain. The verses were short and the words were simple, for it was among simple men that he dwelt. He sang:

"Horse of the pampa run to thy doom.
The gaucho chases after thee and has no mercy
in his heart.

See the blue sky for the last time.
Taste the green grass before dying.

Horse of the pampa race to thy doom.
The birds call thee back but in fear thou dost
    not hear them.
Freedom thou hast lost for ever,
Excepting the freedom of death."

There was silence when he had sung his song and
the gauchos felt sorrow for the horses they had killed.
They loved freedom, as did the horse, they dwelt upon
the same land, shared the same sky and slept upon the
same grass. The horse of the pampa was their brother,
helpmate and friend, and for a while the gauchos were
sad, thinking of the betrayal.

But as the day progressed they forgot. They sliced
themselves mouthfuls of meat from the smoking roasts,
using the same long knives to eat and kill; quenched
their thirsts with crude wine, and grew loud and gay
in their merry-making.

They remembered the four horses in the corral and
rushed to release them one at a time, crowding glee-
fully about the gateway, and they agreed to save La
Bruja until the last, for she was ugly enough to be
made clown for the day.

The first horse dashing for freedom, a three-year-old
colt of piebald coloring, was stopped suddenly in his
flight by boleadoras twisting round his hoofs, which
dragged him to the ground. He sprang to all-fours
again and a lasso fell over his head. In confusion he
became aware of a man upon his back and, squealing
with rage, did his utmost to fling him off. But all his

strength was of no avail. The battle was like those of yesterday except that this colt had more freedom.

He dashed among the yelling gauchos and crushed several naked feet. He fled across the flaming beds of fire and made for the open pampa, but a gaucho on horseback turned him and he galloped back again, all the while aware of the man astride him who laughed and hooted and dug in his spurs. The frantic fight went on until the colt fell down in exhaustion, foaming at the mouth, defeated.

Out came the second horse, galloping to freedom as madly as she could, a dun-colored mare who had borne eight foals on the pampa. She put up only a token fight when a gaucho jumped astride her, for she had a ninth foal within her and was weak with hunger and thirst.

When she was defeated the gauchos opened the gate again and let out the third, a filly in her second year who had little more energy than the mare. She was beautiful, a bay with a white streak down her face and black points, and the man who rode her was gentle, for he did not want to ruin her.

There remained only La Bruja and Thamár and La Bruja shot out of the corral with such fantastic speed that the gauchos were astonished and forgot to bring her down. Thamár galloped valiantly behind her and the gauchos laughed at the amusing spectacle of beautiful daughter trying so vainly to keep apace with her ugly dam.

Thamár fell with the boleadoras tangled about her legs and when she had regained her footing La Bruja was far out of reach, a fast vanishing shadow on the pampa. The gauchos brought the struggling foal to the payador and asked if he would accept her as payment for his song about the horse of the pampa.

The old poet gravely examined the trembling, fawn-like creature, who, too fearful of all the men about her, did not struggle to escape.

"She is very beautiful," said the poet. "Like a princess, and I shall call her Thamár for her beauty."

The gauchos put a rope about her neck and tied one foreleg beneath her chin so that she could not run away, and on three legs she stood and trembled until the day was over, fear, discomfort and hunger her companions. With the coming of night the payador released her leg and tied her to a wagon wheel, saying her name again and again, and she fell asleep with the sound in her ears . . . Thamár.

Chapter 7

FREEDOM AGAIN

I

It was soon that La Bruja realized her loss, but such was her fear of mankind that she dared not return in search of her youngling. She turned back a little way to call her softly, not daring to raise her voice above a nicker for fear that some man would spring out of the grass to take her. In this land of flatness there could be no doubt that Thamár did not follow, for there was neither ridge nor tree to hide her if she came, nor even giant thistles.

Deeply mourned La Bruja for the foal. Never had she been so lonely as she was now and she circled constantly about the place where she had been a prisoner, distant enough for safety but near enough, she believed, to hear any answering cry. But Thamár had gone. The payador stayed only one night more and La Bruja called in vain, her cries stricken with grief and longing.

The gauchos heard and saw her. They recognized the lonely mother as she stood afar off, calling to Thamár, and they wondered at her audacity and her grief. They left her alone, for she was ugly and undesirable as either mount or brood-mare and they were preparing to leave the place, hitching oxen to the wagons, saddling up their horses, stamping out the fires they had made. Let her find new companions and forget Thamár. They had had enough of killing for a while and felt no desire to molest her.

The gauchos, ever nomads, moved away from the place of slaughter and when La Bruja in her desperation came nearer she saw that the place was deserted and decided to explore, though she kept well clear of the empty stockade, fearing it still. What scent there had been of Thamár had long since faded, borne away on the winds, and the lonely mother found nothing to tell her of the foal.

She stayed close to the place for some time, still calling to Thamár and listening with quivering ears for the foal's reply, but no answer ever came to ease her aching loss, only the passing of time which heals all sorrows.

So La Bruja forgot Thamár, though for some time she missed the dancing shadow at her heels, the hungry lips searching for milk, the soft, warm body to caress. While she remembered she moped and became more ugly and even when she forgot her life was empty and she could find no joy.

Winter came and her hair grew thick in gingery patches. She cropped the grass and found a place to drink, but always she grazed alone, near the place of slaughter, for no other horses dwelled nearby.

The winter grass grew through the blood-stained earth and the fat-bellied hawks left few remains. Skulls and ribs grew bleached in the sun and wind and rain, but La Bruja did not recognize them and had no fear of them. She grazed round them as if they were stones, never knowing them as the remains of her companions, and the earth no longer smelled of blood but was fresh with new grass and damp dew.

La Bruja saw no more of men, but she kept a wary watch for them. Although she forgot Thamár, she never forgot the brutalities of man and her heart remained bitter toward him, rankling at what she had seen, heard and smelled.

If La Bruja had been only ugly she would have been completely forgotten by the gauchos, but she possessed the speed of her grandsire and this had not gone unnoticed by one man at least. His name was Gregorio and he had watched La Bruja's flight from the stockade without comment, appraising her with his sharp black eyes, but stolidly chewing a piece of meat. He listened to his companions as they laughed and joked about her and learned that they had only regarded her ugliness, perhaps excusing her speed for fear. They had not considered the length of her legs, the shape of her body, which told Gregorio of her different blood, and he decided that he wanted La Bruja, for what is ugliness when the horse is fleeter than any other?

Gregorio had a job waiting for him at an estancia far distant, and, with several companions, had been employed to drive a herd of cattle to the Brazilian borders. For this reason he could not chase after La Bruja now. But this did not trouble him. He felt certain that La Bruja would not have wandered far from the district in which she dwelt by the time he returned to capture her, and he was prepared to wait.

Gregorio, a tall, thin man of middle years, had

learned patience, knowing that few things in life can be had at once. The money he earned from the cattle-drive would suffice to pay for a good horse and he would need a fast mount if he were to catch La Bruja. He remained silent about his plans, for fear that some other might claim La Bruja also, and while he jogged steadily across the pampa to Brazil, driving skinny, half-wild cattle before him, he kept a picture of the ugly mare in his mind and silently rejoiced with the thought that one day she would be his.

II

Spring came again, the fourth that La Bruja had known, and this time there was no new-born foal at her heels, bleating for milk, for she had dwelt alone all this year. She felt the gladness of the season and her moping heart grew bright again as the summer birds came flocking back to their grassy playground, crying and squawking their greetings as they flew, leaving the northern hemisphere to the bitterness of coming winter.

Thick mists covered the land each new day and the sun shone through them like a brazen ball, glowing fiercely orange, almost red. La Bruja rejoiced in the freshness of the mornings, which were damp and clean and exhilarating. For the first time since the loss of Thamár she was glad again and her spirit swelled within her as she smelled and tasted, felt and heard the hope with which spring came winging over the land.

She spent her new-found energy in racing about the pampa, kicking, twisting, tossing her head, a foal again in her delight. When she galloped the wind blew against her; mane and tail streamed out behind her and she felt the air rushing past her body, glorying in her speed and the thunder of her hoofs over the earth.

Her shaggy winter coat fell away and glossy new hair replaced it, shining even in the dullness of its color. Her eyes grew warm and bright and her angry heart was eased. Excitement filled her and she roamed the pampa restless in her loneliness, the turgid blood of winter no longer creeping through her veins. She drank in the wind with eagerness, searching she knew not what, and one day the scent of her own kind was in the wind.

This was what she wanted, company after so many long months alone. She galloped toward the place from whence the wind came, head high, heart excited, possessed by a spirit she did not understand. She came to new territory in her search, land she had never trod before, but she was aware of no strangeness, eager only to assuage the feeling within her and to find the horse whose scent she had followed for days.

She ate of the fast-growing thistles, becoming fat on their succulent leaves, and she rested but little, for she felt no tiredness. She came suddenly upon the horse whose scent she had followed, drawing back startled as she found him standing among the thistle thickets, watching and waiting for her, for he knew she came.

He was a young stallion with scarcely more than six springs behind him and he surveyed La Bruja with eagerness, his bright eyes sparkling, his small, sharp ears straining toward her. Skewbald in color, he was almost completely white but for a chestnut patch across his rump and a chestnut head, broken only by a triangular patch of whiteness on his muzzle. He had no herd of his own and, as yet, had fought few battles in order to possess mares for himself. He grazed alone without companions and sometimes he followed the rheas or the guanacos when loneliness became overwhelming.

Thus it was with great eagerness that he surveyed the startled mare. He nickered a soft welcome and La Bruja twitched her ears in acknowledgment, fearing too much friendliness. The stallion drew near to her and she stood her ground, quivering as he approached and touched her with his soft, damp muzzle.

Then she returned his greeting and, standing among the thistles, they discovered each other unhurriedly, the spring sun shining warm upon them, crickets chirping in the grass.

Chapter 8

MAN WITHOUT PITY

I

La Bruja and the stallion stayed together. Both lonely creatures, they grew to like each other's company and they grazed daily side by side, the stallion guarding La Bruja with tenderness and zeal. Sometimes he was over-zealous and La Bruja did not like him then, turning on him with bared teeth and flattened ears if he tried to drive her against her will. He learned to respect her independence and each day passed in contentment for them both.

Sometimes they wandered alone in search of food, but they rarely strayed far apart. Together, with curiosity, they watched two stags fighting for possession of each other's hinds and they jumped, involuntarily startled, as the angry antlers clashed again and again. The stags pushed each other back and forth, digging their dainty hoofs with firm force into the earth in order not to give way under pressure, but finally the power of the elder stag prevailed and the young one limped crestfallen away, leaving his hinds to the other.

Handsome cock birds preened their feathers before entranced hens, but sped away startled at the heavy approach of La Bruja and the stallion. Baby guanacos ran beside their mothers, with the same long necks and haughty stares, and their coats were soft and curly, like clean young wool.

La Bruja and the stallion fed greedily upon the thistles and grass and clover. Summer was coming. The air grew hot and sultry, the freshness of the spring months faded and dryness crept slowly over the land. The sap in the thistles began to evaporate, the flowers opened and let loose millions of floating seeds in a last desperate attempt for prolongation of life. The seeds sank to the ground and here the two horses feasted upon them, snaffling them up with their soft upper lips, snorting as they found them in their nostrils, not noticing those which stuck in their manes and tails, and where the seeds remained uneaten there grew thistles the following year.

The grass withered and grew brown. The thistles stood tall, rusty and dead and La Bruja and the stallion no longer fed so well. There were days of constant sunshine, weeks of heat when no wind blew, and then came a session of storms which softened the sun-baked ground and brought freshness once more to the pampa. During all this time La Bruja and the stallion grazed without coming upon another of their kind, for this part of the pampa was almost bereft of horses since the gauchos had done their slaughtering the year before.

There came a day, however, when their sharp ears caught the trembling of hoofs upon the ground and they looked up sharply, fear striking La Bruja, curiosity the stallion's only reaction. Upon the horizon they saw two horses, one of which carried a rider, and this sight was enough for La Bruja. She turned swiftly from where she stood and fled from the approaching traveler. The stallion did not follow her, not understanding her fear.

He stared again at the horses and rider and viewed them with puzzlement, as innocent of man as La Bruja had once been. Then he turned to see where La Bruja had gone and found that she was far distant from him now, not even answering the plaintive cry he sent after her. He remained where he was for one moment more, curiosity and desire to stay with La Bruja struggling one against the other. Eventually he decided in favor of La Bruja and galloped after her, forgetting those who followed, for they had no meaning to him.

The man who followed was Gregorio. He had traveled back and forth across the pampa all that spring and summer searching for La Bruja and at last he had found her. He did not hurry his horses, for he knew that La Bruja would tire herself in panic and then he could take her, for his horses would still be fresh. He smiled to himself as he saw how she ran, appreciating her even from such a distance, for she was soon far away from him in her fear. The horses he had bought were fleet, but with a fleetness not comparable to that of La Bruja. Therefore, Gregorio knew that he must use cunning to catch her, cunning and time.

II

The days that followed filled La Bruja with constant fear, for always on the horizon was the man with his horses. She grew fretful and would not eat, never satisfied until the man was no longer within her sight, needing to run many miles in order to lose him. The stallion could not understand her fear and he tired of her strange behavior. She was too swift for him and one day he did not follow when she bolted again, gazing wistfully after her for a while but no longer prepared to spend each day in such a manner. Some fear of man he had communicated, so that he did not stand and wait for the gaucho's approach but made off in another direction, and for some days his heart was sad because he had lost La Bruja.

La Bruja, alone again, grew more anxious. She had taken comfort from the proximity of the stallion and felt safer when he was near. Now he had deserted her and fear became panic as she realized that she could not escape the man who trailed her.

Southward she fled and behind her came Gregorio, quietly certain of success. La Bruja could feel no security unless she put great distances between herself and him and because of this she traveled constantly throughout the day, galloping until her strained heart stabbed with pain and her legs buckled.

On and on came Gregorio, no pity for the lone wild mare within him. She would be soon within his reach, for he saw how she half staggered at times and noticed that her pace had slowed. How proud he would be of her when she was his. Even her ugliness would be overlooked when his friends saw how she ran. It was a pity that she had not the beauty of her foal, but one could not have everything in this life, and animals, like humans, have usually at least one defect for all their attributes.

La Bruja knew she was beaten. For weeks the man

had followed her, through sun and storm, and she had not outrun him. Her heart was overtaxed, her legs were tired and her growing foal seemed like lead within her. She stared with wild eyes and flattened ears, flanks heaving in distress, and she saw the man draw near with hope dying in her heart, her spirit overwhelmed with fear and hatred.

She turned again to flee and heard fast pounding hoofs not far behind her. She strained with every muscle, fear giving her a strength which did not come from her body. She might have escaped the gaucho even then had he not swung his boleadoras after her and, with deadly aim, entwined them about her hoofs. She crashed to the ground in shock and confusion, not even realizing that the thing round her legs was an invention of man, and when she staggered upward once more a lasso fell over her head and she was a prisoner.

Even now she would not give in. She fought against the rope which held her with all the fury her tired, shaken body could muster. She screamed and reared and savagely shook her head, but the rope grew tight about her throat and nearly choked her. Exhaustion defeated her eventually and she suddenly dropped her hoofs to the ground and stopped fighting, head hanging, tongue lolling from her jaws, swollen and dry.

Gregorio held her in his power and he was confident that she would soon be docile. He could afford to feel kindly disposed toward her now, so he led her gently to a lake which was at some short distance, giving life to a solitary ombú tree, and there La Bruja gladly slaked her thirst, forgetting the man in her eagerness. But she could not forget him for more than an in-

stant, for he held the leather rope which clung to her
throat and commanded her every movement. His
shadow fell across her, like the shadow of the ombú,
and there was a shadow across her heart because she
was his prisoner.

III

La Bruja remained wakeful all the night. She stood
by the lake, occasionally swallowing a mouthful of
water, and the heaviness in her heart did not fade, because not far from her slept the man who had captured her. He had tied her hind legs together, so that
she could do no more than hobble when she moved,
and his two bay geldings dozed not far from him, forgetting their new companion while they slept.

The sky was dark and the moon hidden in a sickly
haze of pallid light. The pampa was alive with a mul-
titude of tiny creatures and La Bruja listened to them,
pricking her ears as she stood beside the lake, involuntarily aware of them. The night seemed long to
the waiting mare and when the gaucho stirred in his
sleep her body trembled and sudden fear rose within
her. Nocturnal insects and cicadas busied themselves
beneath the branches of the ombú where the gaucho
slept and La Bruja was aware of them too, aware of
everything in that endless night.

How lonely she felt and afraid. She stared at the two
geldings, wondering at their calm acceptance of man,
their docility. They were completely incomprehensible
to her and even though she saw these two of her kind
unafraid she could not believe that the man would not

hurt her. The fear and hatred she had learned in that stockade of death remained in her memory and returned to torment her now. The night was long while she awaited her fate and she could not sleep for fear of it.

The sun rose and it was a feeble sun, so that from early morning the sky was overcast with grayness and a chill wind blew, tugging at La Bruja's ragged tail and mane, rustling among the thickly leaved branches of the tree. She nibbled without hunger at the grass and ignored the nickered greetings of the two geldings, fearing them, too, as creatures of man.

Gregorio awoke and he let La Bruja see how he patted his mounts and spoke to them with kindness. She trembled for them when his hands touched their bodies, but they did not seem concerned and one even pushed his head toward the gaucho, as if begging more attention.

With the coming of dawn the rodents had vanished to their underground retreats, the insects had faded with the darkness, and, apart from the birds which inhabited the lakeside, the three horses and Gregorio were alone on the pampa, which was swathed in gray dullness and by its very drabness portended sadness or evil.

The weather did not disturb the gaucho. He felt the warmth of his shabby, gaily striped poncho and he pulled his hat well down over the handkerchief round his head and neck. He wore new leather boots, the heels of which sparkled with silver spurs, and on these and the horses he had spent his money.

Gregorio had proved his patience by the way in

which he had waited his time before setting out to capture La Bruja and by the way in which he trailed her
once he had found her again. He had spent many days
in the chase and his reward was the mare, which he
knew he could never have captured by ordinary meth-
ods. But now that La Bruja was in his hands his patience fled away. He was like a child who must play
with his new toy at once and on this drab and chilly
morning he was determined to ride the mare until she
accepted him, anxious to feel her power under his command, eager to race with her as she stretched her long
legs in flight across the pampa.

Already La Bruja was trembling, divining his intentions, so Gregorio gave her time to calm herself while
he prepared maté, the tea-like herb so favored by the
gaucho, which would sustain him until he had a proper
meal. He carried his kettle slung beneath the belly of
one of his horses, tied to its girth, and only a few minutes had passed by the time he had lighted a small
fire, filled the kettle with water from the lake and
waited for it to boil.

La Bruja watched all these preparations with fear
and bewilderment, translating everything the gaucho
did into portending evil. She watched the steam rise
from the kettle and disappear into the air; she saw the
gaucho sit down beside the fire when he had made the
maté, sucking it from a bowl through a thin metal tube,
and Gregorio watched her too. He saw that her trembling ceased, but he saw fear and hatred in her white-
ringed eyes and he did not underestimate his opponent.

The dullness of the day became more profound as

time passed and all the surrounding pampa lay under
the same gray cloud. Beyond the other side of the lake
there was little to be seen but occasional stalks of rushes
which towered jaggedly above their fellows. The wild
birds were strangely silent, perhaps subdued by the
nearness of man. The breath of the three horses and the
man hung upon the air then vanished and there was
not a sound but for the occasional rustle of a bird in
the rushes or the impatient stamp of a hoof.

Gregorio's patience lasted no longer. Before he had
been all slowness, but now he showed a deceptive
speed in the way he released La Bruja's hind legs and,
a second later, flung himself upon her back, gathering
up the lasso as he did so. Breaking a horse alone was
a risky business, for if he should be thrown La Bruja
might escape him. He determined to hold fast upon the
lasso about her neck, not intending to lose her after
spending so much time in capturing her.

He was hardly upon her back when the fight began.
The silence of the morning was crudely broken, for La
Bruja was like any other wild horse in her fear of the
body clinging suddenly to her. Her remembrance of the
clinging puma came back to her and it seemed to her
that man must be akin to the lion and she bucked and
reared with savage fury, eyes rolling, ears flat, teeth
bared.

Gregorio was no mean rider and he bore with all La
Bruja's tricks, encouraging her to fight more furiously
and tire rapidly.

La Bruja that morning seemed tireless. She flung herself back and forth squealing as her rage increased,

rage mingled with desperation because she could not win.

Gregorio laughed and swore and urged her more, feeling tiredness creeping into her. She no longer flung her head so high, her bucks grew weaker and her rearings were but feeble protestations. For all this, however, she would not give in, for the freedom of the pampa, which today was lost beneath a canopy of grayness, was in her blood and her wild heart was strong within her.

The grief for her stolen foal, the sight and smell of slaughtered horses, the malice she had borne toward mankind ever since; all these things, forgotten in actuality, had become part of her instinct and she fought now because violent instinct made her fight and the man upon her back was death to her if she could not defeat him.

Instinct died in weariness; trembling legs and beaten body could fight no more; savage spirit was quelled by gasping lungs and panting heart. La Bruja fell beneath the gaucho's weight and lay almost lifeless in the grass, jaws apart, eyes staring, legs stiff.

Gregorio, who had sprung aside as he felt her collapsing, looked down upon her with consternation. He put his hand upon her swollen neck and a shudder passed through La Bruja's body. No, she was not dead, though her eyes were glazed and her tongue lolled out. Gregorio tied her legs again and left her to recover.

He made up the dead fire and sat beside it, rolling himself a cigarette as he waited. He inhaled the warm, bitter smoke with slow pleasure, needing himself to relax, for La Bruja's fight had been no mean one and he was tired too. His bay geldings returned to grazing, after watching fearfully the struggle between La Bruja and their master, and after a while, hunger overcoming all else, they forgot the exhausted mare.

The lasso greatly hampered her movements.

Chapter 9

THE WILD HEART

I

Gregorio smoked three cigarettes before La Bruja stirred. She sat up slowly, struggling a while before achieving this much, and for a long time she attempted no more than this, exhaustion still overcoming her. How ugly she looked in her weariness, her coloring in keeping with the funereal aspect of the daylight. Her tired head drooped to the grass and she had not even the energy to snort when a few blades tickled her nostrils. She did not attempt to rise to all-fours and for the rest of the day stayed as she was, ignoring the gaucho as if he did not exist.

Gregorio left her in peace. He took a horse and went in search of food, a deer perhaps which he could bring down with his boleadoras, sure that while he was gone La Bruja would make no attempt to escape him. Neither did she, and her heart was not even gladdened by his absence, for she was too weary to care for anything.

The day and night passed and the next dawn brought new light to the pampa, pushing away the grayness with warm, bright sunshine. La Bruja felt freshened and she was on her feet before the gaucho woke, hunger driving her to eat greedily, although sadness had returned to her heart. Fear had died. The gaucho had done all he could and she had survived him. Still she was a prisoner, but her sadness was broken by a rising spirit of anger as tiredness fell away and freshness came to her again.

Gregorio came a second time to ride her and was surprised by the fury with which she greeted him. He had considered her broken after yesterday's fight, but found her spirited and perhaps more bitter than before. The battle began again and La Bruja learned trickery as she fought, turning with snapping teeth to grab at the gaucho's leg and rolling suddenly on the ground. But Gregorio was ready for all her tricks and she did not take him unawares.

He thrashed her head severely when she tried to bite him; he jumped aside when she rolled, but was upon her back again before she could rise and escape him. When she tried to crush his leg against the trunk of the ombú he retaliated so severely that she thought better of it and did not try again.

But La Bruja would not admit defeat and again she fell down in exhaustion before Gregorio could break her. She lay as if dead and the gaucho realized that he would never break her spirit, at least not in this way. While she recovered he sat and thought, wanting to keep this mare alive, for he valued greatly the speed she had shown. If he could not defeat her he must either kill or release her, for she herself would accept no other alternative.

Another day's riding like this would kill her. Then all his long months of hoping would be wasted. There must be some other way to defeat her, but he did not know it. On the pampa a horse was tamed by brute force, by spur and whip and strength, and Gregorio knew no other way.

While he drank maté, ate meat and slept in the afternoon sun, his saddle for a pillow, his poncho for a blanket, La Bruja gradually regained strength.

Through her blind, staring eyes the sun suddenly pierced. Scents returned to her nostrils, sounds came to her ears, and with this return to feeling came the ache of her weary body, bruised and cut by the weapons of man. The healing grazes of the day before were freshly opened, the bruises newly aggravated. What stiffness and what dizziness she felt as she lifted her head, feeling the sun upon her which beat down strongly in midafternoon.

She staggered to her feet and found it less difficult than on the previous occasion, for the gaucho had forgotten to hobble her. Her legs were free, but she had not the energy to run far, and run she must if she wished to escape, for there was no hiding place on this flat land, bereft of all camouflage but that of distance.

The gaucho slept soundly, hat upon his face to keep the sun from his eyes, and he was unaware of La Bruja's recovery. The sun lulled him sweetly in its heat and he knew nothing.

Seeing him lying there, apparently helpless, for he was not upon his feet, all the bitterness and violence and pain surged into La Bruja's heart again and she hated the gaucho with unparalleled hatred, filled with desire to destroy him. Unafraid now, reckless in her desperation, she approached the sleeping man and the scent of him filled her with a madness and fear such as that which had struck her when the puma had attacked her so long ago.

She let out a wild scream of rage and the gaucho woke with a start to find her naked front hoofs rearing over him. He gave a cry of fear and with the speed of a snake rolled from where he lay, but this time La Bruja was quicker. One hoof crashed upon the ground. The second landed heavily upon the softness of Gregorio's body and he grunted with surprised pain as he felt it, too stunned for greater exclamation.

Again and again La Bruja attacked the gaucho and he lay helpless beneath her vicious hoofs until all life was crushed from him and the violence that surged through La Bruja was satisfied.

For the second time in her life she had killed, but this time she had killed a man.

II

La Bruja could not forget the killing of the man as she had forgotten the killing of the puma. Although she roamed far from the place of death, so that the ombú was not even within sight, the memory of what had occurred there rankled constantly within her. Perhaps it was because she had killed the puma with nothing but fear to spur her, whereas hatred had driven her to kill the man, even when he was not actually molesting her.

That hatred was with her still, smarting in her heart as the weals on her body smarted. The cuts of the spurs and the lashes of the rope healed upon her skin, but the soreness in her heart did not fade, so that she was constantly aware of a burning anger, even though she knew that the gaucho could harm her no more.

Although she had killed, still she had not completely freed herself from man's influence, for there was the lasso about her neck and it trailed in the grass beside her while she grazed.

For many days she tried to rid herself of the rope. She shook her head from side to side, she stamped on it with her death-giving hoofs, and grew wild with rage when everything she did was to no avail. As time passed she grew accustomed to the feel of it about her neck and almost forgot it, but there were occasions when she trod on it while grazing, or when it tangled itself about her legs or about a clump of weeds, tugging at her as once the man had tugged, putting wild fear into her heart until she realized that it was not a man who held her.

The lasso greatly hampered her movements, so that she could no longer gallop without fear of falling or being caught up in thistles or long grass and, after many frustrations of this kind, she spent one entire afternoon chewing through a section of it, making it shorter but not removing it, the latter being her original intention. However, it was short enough after that not to trail on the ground and, though it swung constantly below her head, she ignored it and after a while accepted it as if it were part of her body.

The days passed by uneventfully. No more men came to molest La Bruja and some of her wild anger faded. She grew more calm but never relaxed her vigilant watch of the horizon and the slightest shadow was enough to set her racing in the opposite direction.

But La Bruja had few desires to hurry in these days and it was only fear that pushed her to a gallop now and then. She had suffered much in the hands of Gregorio and her body was still tired.

When the cold fingers of winter began to stretch across the pampa in gusts of wind and icy rain La Bruja hunched her body and suffered the coldness, not having the energy to journey northward as she had done in previous years. With each succeeding day she felt more worn and there came a morning when she knew that her foal would be born even though winter had hardly come and spring was far away.

She could find no shelter on the plain, for the new thistles had not grown and the old had fallen. She could muster no desire to search farther afield, so she stood where she was until the foal was born. The pampa was soggy with rain and La Bruja's head drooped in misery.

The foal was born without life and La Bruja did no more than sniff at it once before turning away, feeling nothing. She hurried away from the place of birth, as she had done the last time, but now there was no second Thamár to follow her and she was lonely.

Throughout the whole winter La Bruja lacked strength and energy. She endured coldness and rain with surprising passivity, stirring only to graze and seeming not to feel the heavy showers upon her skinny body. She was gaunt and graceless in appearance, even more the scarecrow with the tattered rope dangling below her head, and winter hair grew in rough, uneven patches.

With each succeeding day of winter new grass came to the pampa and with it came new energy to La Bruja. The first fresh grass was weak and tasteless, but as it grew in strength and rapidity, covering the deserted pampa with new life, La Bruja ate more greedily until she had no need to search for fresh grass among the old. Then she settled down to leisurely grazing and as the spring grew closer once again her weakness faded, her old energy returned and she was strong again.

Flesh came to her thin neck and ribby flanks. She lifted her head and gazed with brighter eyes upon her world, but now her eyes were marked with a bitterness which had not existed in the previous spring and she had the look of vice. Her winter coat fell away and a gloss came once more to her hide, a hide now marked with small, uneven scars where the spurs of the gaucho had cut her deep.

The sun grew warmer and came earlier every day, following fleecy clouds which glowed with touches of gold in a pale and silver sky. The warmth and the freshness of the new spring mornings gave La Bruja gladness once again, though she was not among the mares that gave new life to the earth, and for a second year she had no youngling to run beside her.

La Bruja listened to the pipits as they caroled in the sky; she heard the plover and the lapwings chorusing the same message and she felt again, as always, the excitement brought by spring. But this year, though she searched the grass and wind, she could find no scent of horses and she wandered solitarily about the pampa, seeking groups of guanaco and deer, flocks of birds, but finding not a single horse for company.

When the first fever of spring passed away La Bruja did not mind that she was without companions and she felt no loneliness. The teasing gusts of wind were company enough and she kicked up her heels in new delight, tossed her head and stretched out her legs to gallop once again, forgetting that she had been galloping in fear for so long, remembering only the thrill of the race.

Somehow, for all her ugliness, La Bruja seemed beautiful when she galloped thus. Her mane and tail flowed behind her, her long legs moved with grace and precision, her spirit soared like the flight of a bird into the blue sky, enhancing her ugly head as it gave a brilliance to her dark eyes, white-ringed though they were.

Left alone, La Bruja could have found contentment on the pampa; happiness in the grass, the sky and the wind; and she would have forgotten the evil of man and her hatred of him. But in her destruction of man she had cut off her hope for happiness and a life unmolested, for now she was spoken of from place to place. Already a man had coveted her for the one thing that gave her happiness and it would not be long before she should be coveted again.

Chapter 10

FELIPE

I

The death of Gregorio was discovered by two travelers who stopped for shelter at the solitary ombú. They journeyed that way only four days later and the gaucho's bay geldings watched with pricked ears as the riders cantered toward them, not understanding the events of the last few days but knowing that their master was dead. Trained in obedience, they had not wandered far from the lake and the ombú, and the sight of them grazing alone in the shadow of the tree was curious to the passing gauchos.

Dusk was gathering gloomily overhead as they reined in their weary horses, but still it was not too dark for them to see the crumpled body which lay beside the saddle and the poncho, damp with the vapors of the earth. They uttered exclamations of surprise at the sight before them, hurriedly dismounting, although they knew that they had come too late.

The way that Gregorio had died was not difficult to ascertain. The whole story was written in the trampled grass and broken ground, and the travelers, surveying the scene, soon understood what had happened.

They examined Gregorio's property; little enough, for all his wealth he carried in his saddlebags and belt like the travelers who found him. They admired his new, mud-streaked boots and fingered his silver spurs, for neither of them possessed boots and their spurs were rusted iron. They discovered that there was no lasso among his property, a thing unusual, for the gaucho is a herder of cattle and the lasso is the instrument of his trade. Because of this they assumed that the killer horse must still have the lasso about its neck and by this sign they should know it if they began a search.

The travelers that night felt no inclination to begin a search. The weather was bad and endless days on the pampa searching a killer horse, which had probably fled far from the district, was not a tempting proposition. Instead they made a fire and slept beneath the tree and when the morning dawned gray and cloudy they tied the dead man to the back of one of his horses and continued their way to the town, speculating on the fury of the killer horse and as to the man's identity.

In the town they discovered more, for it was there that Gregorio had bought his two bay geldings.

"He said he wanted two fleet-footed horses, for he was after the fastest horse he had ever seen."

This the horse-dealer told to the travelers and there was a quickening of interest in the eyes of all the listeners. Many heard his words, for they stood together in the pulpería, a combination of tavern, store and meeting place, and they leaned against barrels of flour or sat on sacks of potatoes, listening while smoking or drinking.

"Is that all he said?" questioned one of the travelers, a youth scarcely bearded but with eyes as sharp as the hawk.

"Little more. He did not seem eager to share his secret. All he would say was that the horse he sought was faster than any other and that he had waited a year to catch her."

"A mare!"

The exclamation was simultaneous upon every lip. None had thought that the killer could be a mare. There was a moment's silence while they digested this information. What kind of a creature must she be that the gaucho waited a year to capture her then died in his attempt to break her? It ill-became any gaucho to ride a mare, so that this one must be something special that he would sacrifice so much.

"Faster than any other," reiterated one at last.

"And he waited a year to catch her," reminded another.

Then the man behind the counter spoke. He had listened unobtrusively to the conversation, counting money, checking off lists of goods, and when he chose he was not conspicuous, for the lighting was bad in the pulpería and there was a thick iron grill between himself and the customers.

"I remember the man," he commented, and he was instantly the center of attention. "He was here a year ago after rounding up horses for the traders. I heard him say that he was going to Brazil. I didn't expect to find him here again like this."

"A year ago," repeated the young traveler thoughtfully. "Then he must have first seen the mare here. He waited a year to capture her. It adds up to that, does it not?"

"Perhaps he saw her at the roundup," added another.

"I was there too and not all the mares were killed. I recall one that escaped, an ugly brute. She looked like a witch. Strangely enough, she had a beautiful colt. We gave it to a payador, I remember."

"Then this must be the one."

The eyes of the young man gleamed. He drew closer to the gaucho who recalled so much and asked him, "Do you remember what she looked like?"

"Well . . . only that she was ugly and almost the color of the earth."

"Then that's enough," said the youth. "We know she's fast, we know she has a rope about her neck, we know she's ugly and dark in coloring. I am going to find her."

"And when you've found her?" questioned another.

"I'm going to ride her."

There was a snort of laughter at this and the man spoke again.

"Son, you only came out of the cradle a year ago. You haven't the experience to ride a horse like that."

"You know nothing about me," returned the youth, and there was anger sparking in his Indian eyes, so that the other, a fat barber of the town, decided to concede him the point.

"Very well," he retorted genially. "Go ahead and find her. Bring her back to town if you can. We'd all like to see this witch. If you succeed I'll teach you how to shave."

The youth made no reply. He pulled a coin from his belt and slammed it down on the counter to pay for the drinks he had taken. He saluted his friend but no other, and left the pulpería with anger and hurt pride

mingled smarting within him. He left his own horse
tied to the rail beside that of his friend and he took the
bay geldings of Gregorio, determined to seek La Bruja
alone.

"I will find her and I will ride her," he muttered to
himself, as he slapped the horses into a gallop, and he
headed toward the ombú beside the lake where
Gregorio had been killed, there intending to begin his
quest.

II

Daylight was failing as Felipe cantered toward the
tree. Gray clouds clung together and were flecked with
flames of red as the sun slowly faded behind them. The
grass became dark, the tree lost its greenness, and the
land was all one shadow beneath the reluctant glow of
a feckless moon. The pampa seemed to be deserted,
but Felipe knew that it was not so, for he had dwelt
all of his sixteen years in this land and knew it, with all
its moods and changes, better than he knew himself.

His naked feet had felt the damp coolness of the
grass and had suffered the cruel stings of thistles lurk-
ing in its softness. With his own hands he had struggled
vainly against the burrowing armadillo and learned
that the smaller creature can have the greater strength.
His face was brown from birth and his eyes black, for
a fair skin would be scorched by the sun and wind,
and he hardly remembered that the sky was not his
natural roof nor the earth his bed, for he had been
orphaned by Indians at an early age and since then no
one had offered him a home.

His first memories were of herding sheep for a rich man. He wore a jacket of sheepskin then, and smelled like the animals he guarded, for he lived among them day and night, ate their flesh and drank their milk. One day the man gave him money for his work. With this he bought a horse and took to herding cattle, but in all his life he could not remember a home nor the face of a kindly woman. He knew cattle and horses and sheep and the rough life of the men of the pampa, but he knew nothing of tenderness or a bed, for such things he had never encountered.

The sun vanished before Felipe reached his destination, but there was light enough by the moon to illuminate his path. The squat, widespread tree loomed ominously in its solitude and the moonlight glinted upon the disturbed waters of the lake as night prowlers came to drink or swim.

Felipe dismounted beside the lake and unsaddled the horse, tying both geldings to a low hanging branch before settling himself, with saddle and poncho, among the roots of the tree, wriggling and twisting until his position was comfortable. The ground below the tree was bare of grass, for many travelers stopped here to rest and when they had gone too little sunlight filtered through the heavy leaves, giving the grass no encouragement to grow again.

Felipe listened to the horses as they blew softly through their nostrils and moved about before sleeping. He heard rustlings in the grass beyond the shadow of the tree as pampa rodents went about their business, and a night bird cried sharply in sudden alarm, startling the boy, although he had often heard the cry before.

He gazed upon the spot where Gregorio had been
found a week earlier and shuddered involuntarily at the
memory. In his mind folklore, legend and Christian religion were strangely mixed and he believed in ghosts
and spirits, thinking that perhaps the ghost of the dead
man hung about the tree, for his manner of death had
been brutal.

He turned his thoughts to La Bruja, for it was not
good to think of ghosts alone. He wondered where she
was at this moment, far or near; what she did and why
she had killed Gregorio. He wished that La Bruja
were a stallion, for then the glory of capturing her and
defeating her would be far greater. Still, he would be
proud enough if he caught her, so he let the wish pass
him by.

She was ugly, one man said, like a witch. This was
misfortune, too. For a moment Felipe doubted the wis-
dom of his decision. Surely it was folly to chase after
an ugly mare. Supposing her speed was but a fantasy?
If it should be so then he would have nothing to show
for his pains. Then he remembered the scorn of the fat
barber and was reassured. He would capture La Bruja
if only to save his pride, and it was Felipe who first
gave her this name.

Felipe was awakened by a spattering of raindrops
upon his face. He started in surprise, for they were
large and icy, and he suddenly remembered where he
was and why, as he saw the cavern-like branches above
him whose leaves bowed under the weight of water.
He scrambled up, stretched his cold and stiffened muscles, and wandered sleepily to the lakeside. The pampa

was shrouded in a mist of grayness and he felt the dampness of the morning clinging to him through his clothes.

It was no day to begin his search, for in such a mist as this the mare could easily elude him. He cursed and kicked the ground, for with the impetuosity of youth it seemed that a century must pass before he would find the trail of La Bruja, if a trail existed after so many days.

With one thought only he consoled himself. If the mare which escaped from the stockade and that which killed Gregorio were one and the same, she had obviously dwelt within this region for much of her life and looked upon it as her home. Therefore the chances were that she would still be within a few leagues of the lake, unless she had taken great fright at her actions and fled to another part.

The boy made himself believe that this was not so. A man must have a certain amount of luck with everything and he felt sure that he would be lucky enough to find La Bruja near within a week or two.

As he stood and thought these things, rain began to fall again. It hissed down finely all about him and Felipe returned to the shelter of the ombú, whose branches were thick enough to guard him from all but an occasional trickle. He collected together a few fallen twigs and added them to the remains of Gregorio's fire. Very soon he started a flame and he crouched down beside it, warming himself, the gloom of the morning somewhat dispersing at this small comfort.

He would let the horses rest and shelter himself for the day. Perhaps on the morrow the sun would shine.

He hoped so because, once he left the shade of the ancient ombú, there would be no more shelter on the pampa and if it rained he could not even light a fire to dry his sodden clothes. But the thought of La Bruja inspired him to take the risk. The dead gaucho had said that she was the fastest horse he had ever seen and, if this were so, she was worth chasing after.

Chapter 11

THE CAPTIVES

I

Felipe's quest appeared from the start to be doomed to failure and bad luck followed him wherever he rode. The depression of the weather seemed interminable and every dawn came weakly to the sky, hardly breaking through the blackness of the preceding night. The sun was without warmth or kindness and the new winter grass grew long and heavy in its wealth of wetness, for there was hardly a day without rain.

While La Bruja gave birth to her lifeless foal, Felipe pulled his horses into the grass and sheltered between them, shivering with cold, no longer caring to wipe the rain from his face as it streamed down upon him. The geldings bowed their heads and bore the icy wind and rain, accustomed to obey the whims of their master, though they would not have lain on the soggy ground from choice. Only will-power kept Felipe to his hopeless task, for never in a single day did he sight La Bruja, and he suffered much for his pride.

There were days when hunger made him weak. The animals on the pampa saw him coming from a distance and they fled from his reach before he could be among them. He caught a bird which he found fluttering feebly on the grass with a broken wing and because he could light no fire he had to eat the flesh raw. There were days when he was numb with cold and his naked feet were like marble. But never did he think of abandoning his quest, for he knew that La Bruja must be near and that only misfortune drove them to take paths in different directions.

Eventually the weather cleared. The sun shone with warmth as well as light and the wet clothes began to dry upon Felipe's back as he rode. Warmth came to his body again, his frozen limbs began to feel and his spirits rose.

He came unawares upon a group of rheas and was among them before they realized his presence, fleeing in a mad panic to escape him, wings flapping, necks outstretched, ugly eyes bulging. He laughed and let them run for a moment, hastily unwinding the boleadoras about his waist. Then with a loud yell he set his horse at a gallop and raced after them, whirling the boleadoras above his head. Sure of his prey, a scraggy brown female that lagged behind, he let his weapon fly and she collapsed in a heap as it entangled her legs, doomed in a moment to death.

Felipe made a fire that day and fed well upon the rhea. What flesh he did not eat he crudely smoked and packed away in his saddlebags for another day. Then he began again his search for the elusive mare, hopes high and stomach filled, certain that one day he would find her.

Spring came. Felipe shared the gladness that was in the air and all about him, for he loved the song of the birds and the colors of the butterflies, although he led a life so rough. He was as aware as a poet might be of the beauties of nature and his heart sang in tune

with the rhythm of spring, putting a sparkle into his
eyes and a grin upon his lips.

One day he saw La Bruja. There was no doubt as to
her identity, for she was ugly as the man had said; she
looked almost black in the distance, and a fraying rope
swung below the level of her breast. She saw him in
the same instant and simultaneously they broke into a
gallop, La Bruja flooded with fear, Felipe rejoicing.

The boy rejoiced too soon. Ill luck was his companion still and, as he urged the gelding to greater speed
with spurs and whip, he was suddenly thrown forward,
the horse collapsed beneath him and Felipe spun
dizzily to the ground, gasping with pain and surprise
as he hit the earth.

The horse scrambled up first, but Felipe saw with
dismay that he lifted one foot from the ground and
rubbed his nose against it. Felipe was shaken and
bruised but otherwise unhurt. He picked himself up
and looked about, seeing at less than a length's distance the rodent hole over which the gelding had
fallen.

The horse was timid in his pain and shied away
when Felipe approached to examine him, but after a
while he submitted to the touch of expert hands, uttering short nickers of pain. There was no doubt that the
fetlock was broken and Felipe cursed his misfortune
when success had been so near.

He unharnessed the gelding, transferring saddle and
bridle to the other horse, glad that he still had the
two. He stroked the lame horse for a moment, then
mounted again and looked about for La Bruja. By now

she was no more than a speck of darkness on the horizon, but at least she was still within sight.

He kicked the second gelding to a gallop and called back to the other, "Goodbye, old friend, and good luck."

The horse pricked his ears and watched him go, bewildered and not understanding. He was free of the trappings of servitude, but he could remember no other life and had no desire for freedom. He began to follow Felipe, cantering awkwardly until pain forced him to halt. He whinnied shrilly after his fast-fleeing companions and it was a cry of longing to be with them.

For a long time he watched them, half expecting them to turn back. They did not return and Felipe called no more. The pricked ears of the gelding drooped and he touched his broken fetlock once again, but it was not within his power to heal it. He dropped his head to graze, holding his hoof from the ground, and eventually he forgot Felipe and the other gelding, waiting on the pampa until fate should resolve his future.

The nightmare in La Bruja's life began again. Followed always by Felipe, she knew no peace, no rest and though he never drew near enough to threaten her he was constantly there. She grazed scantily, snatching mouthfuls of grass and clover with flattened ears and gleaming eyes, pausing in her stride for no more than ten minutes at a time. She watched the boy on horseback with bitter hatred, but although she ranged far from his sight she could not lose him.

He was not insistent like Gregorio. With only one horse to bear him, Felipe was held back and could not press the pace, for the gelding tired more quickly than La Bruja, who carried no extra weight. Therefore he could do no more than follow her as the moon follows the sun, day in, day out, never narrowing the gap between them but never losing ground either.

Following her thus, watching her fear and desperation, a feeling of friendship toward her began to grow in Felipe. He had searched for her long and constantly, his mind filled with thoughts of her from dawn till dusk, and now that he saw her every day his desire to capture her faded and he held only a desire to gain her confidence.

He saw how she watched him while she ate, head held high as her jaws worked hungrily, and as he slowly closed in upon her she would shake her head as if in anger, turn about and race away. As time passed her reactions became slower. She allowed him closer and did not run so far. Either she was gaining in confidence toward him or she was growing reckless because he had not harmed her. Whatever the cause, Felipe's heart was glad. With patience he might one day draw near enough to rope her and then she would be his.

Following her thus, his every thought concentrated in gaining the trust of this ugly, elusive mare, Felipe lost count of the days he traveled and the direction in which La Bruja led him. The sun was warm upon his back and he was aware only of the blueness of the sky, the growing thistles and the cane-brakes. He felt

no lack of human companionship and when he needed
to give voice he spoke to his horse and sometimes
called to La Bruja. The sound of his voice was enough
to set her off again with shaking head and tossing mane,
and Felipe laughed to see her fear, for the chase had
become almost a game to him. He forgot that he had
once been in earnest and that La Bruja had killed a
man.

La Bruja led him southward. Her native land seemed
no longer safe to her and fear drove her to search new
pastures. She trod strange ground, but she could not
shake off her follower. She ate new grasses and sometimes searched for days in thirst for water, in these
new lands not knowing where lakes or rivers were. The
ground became more undulating and the horizons were
no longer empty but shadowed by vague, blue hills.
Wherever she trod the grass was green and plentiful,
for spring was over all the land and there was no lack
of pasturage.

Apart from La Bruja, the gelding and Felipe, the
pampa was almost deserted. At times they passed herds
of guanacos, bunches of deer and several straying cattle, but they came across no human habitations for La
Bruja kept well clear of these. If she saw distant smoke,
or smelled the scent of man on the wind, she changed
direction instantly, and the more she hurried southward the less inhabited the land became.

Only Felipe La Bruja could not escape, but now,
after so many days and nights, his presence worried
her less, for he seemed not eager to molest her. At
times she almost forgot that he followed her, but when

she heard his voice or saw him spur his gelding to a gallop she fled before him, filled with fear and hatred once again. She could not forget Gregorio.

II

One day both Felipe and La Bruja were startled. The morning had been quiet, broken only by the chirping of birds and the sound of the horses as they cropped the grass, when suddenly there was a pounding of hoofs to the west of them where the ground sloped steeply away, as if it were a plateau on which La Bruja grazed. Even as their attention was drawn, three wild horsemen topped the rise in the ground and with loud, inhuman screeches bore down upon them, waving fronded spears and whirling boleadoras.

They were Indians, with black hair to their shoulders and half-naked bodies gleaming. One glance sufficed Felipe. Fear leapt into his heart as he jerked his gelding round and thudded its flanks with his spurs. The gelding caught his fear and needed no urging. The fiendish screams of the half-naked savages were enough to drive him to an extent beyond Felipe's capabilities and even La Bruja, trapped between the two, chose the evil she knew and followed the boy. She soon overtook him, flinging out her long legs with grace and incredible speed and, as the thundering hoofs and fiercesome screams grew louder, Felipe longed to be astride her, for she ran like the wind far ahead of him.

The Indian ponies, fresh and wild, soon overtook the gelding and Felipe was jerked roughly from the saddle

by a lasso about his body. The Indians, too, had seen
the speed of La Bruja and they uttered excited words
while they galloped along, still dragging the boy behind them, agreeing to capture her too. The savage
who had ensnared Felipe drew his pony to a halt and
his two companions raced after La Bruja, their boleadoras whistling above their heads as they prepared to
let them fly.

La Bruja, galloping with open mouth and flecked
with foam, dodged the first flung boleadoras, but the
second, following swiftly, caught her about the fetlocks and she turned a somersault as she fell. The
Indians gave a cry of delight as she struggled to all-
fours. They both swung a lasso about her and for the
third time she was a prisoner.

Felipe saw what happened. Though racked with
pain and breathless, he watched the progress of his
mare, for he thought of La Bruja as his mare. The
Indian, short, flat-nosed and ugly, saw his interest,
staring at him with black, unfeeling eyes, and he made
signs for Felipe to mount his horse again, pointing with
his long spear to the saddle.

Stiffly, Felipe did as he was commanded and
strangely enough some of his fear had faded. He was
more sad than afraid, angry that the Indians should
steal his horse after he had followed her for so long.
He watched while the other Indians returned to their
companion, La Bruja struggling vainly between them,
and he hated them for the triumphant grins on their
ugly faces because it was his triumph that they had
stolen.

The night was sultry and dark. Heavy clouds banked themselves in front of the moon, glowing with eerie light, blue and yellow and silver. The stars seemed distant, hardly visible with no moon to illuminate them, and the Indian encampment was a mass of obscurity, black and shadowless.

Felipe, lying prostrate on the ground, had feigned unconsciousness for hours. His arms and legs were knotted with cramp and only fear of what the Indians might do, once they discovered him conscious, had kept him from crying out. Now all was silent. He had listened without moving until voices died, fires were extinguished and footsteps faded. He knew only that he was on the outskirts of this village of tents and that horses were corraled nearby. The one thing which had been burning in his mind all this time, making each hour drag into days, was the knowledge that La Bruja was among these horses, for he had seen the Indians put her there.

While he lay in the dirt for hours, his body unmoving, his mind worked speedily, making and rejecting plans of escape. In his heart he knew that he was doomed, for the Indian could be likened to a cat with a mouse, playing with retracted claws until the game grew boring. Then . . . Felipe shuddered. The Indians were experts when it came to inflicting a lingering death.

So he thought of escape and he thought of La Bruja, and soon he thought of escape *with* La Bruja. He needed a horse with wings to outrun a horde of Indians, and La Bruja was his only hope. He knew that she was wild, untamed, unridable, but if fate were on his side she might tolerate him upon her back, in the gladness of being free from the corral. He remembered how he had told the barber he would ride her and even in his present plight he felt a surge of pride that the opportunity had come at last for him to try.

He judged the clouds and the moon behind them, deciding that he must act soon if darkness were to be his cover. Slowly, agonizingly, he pulled his throbbing body into action, wriggling toward the corral with wildly thumping heart. The horses stirred and snorted. Felipe halted. He slowly raised his head and searched for La Bruja, seeing with relief that she stood with drooping head beside the bars, the old lasso still about her.

He found the entrance to the corral, still wriggling snake-like on the ground, and he risked raising himself enough to open the gate. The horses grew more restless, their sharp ears picking up every sound as Felipe crawled about the corral. Now that the gate was open there was nothing more for him to do but run to La Bruja, jump astride her and hope that she would carry him to freedom.

For a moment he held back, as if in that instant he realized all that he would lose if his actions failed. In his short sixteen years his life had been hard, but he had known contentment and his pampa home was a place he loved. He could choose another horse, one already accustomed to a rider, and his chances of escape would be even.

Some instinct made him choose La Bruja, the wild mare for whom he felt great affection. Strange circumstances had led him to follow her so far and he would not forsake her now. If he could not have her no man would, and he dashed suddenly to her, vaulted on to her back and whispered urgently, "Let's go."

La Bruja went. Startled, she fled through the open gateway, followed by four or five others, and the noise they made as they whinnied surprise and pounded away from the encampment with galloping hoofs, brought half a dozen Indians from their tents, shouting and gesticulating. One more alert than the rest, threw himself upon an escaping pony, grabbed a spear which leaned against his tent and followed in angry pursuit.

At that moment, after struggling long to probe a pathway through the clouds, the moon shone out in all its brilliance, illuminating the pampa with sudden light, the final ill luck of Felipe.

The Indian grunted with satisfaction as he raised his spear and within a second it had left his practiced hand and found its target, toppling Felipe soundlessly from La Bruja. The mare, suddenly free of the unaccustomed body, pricked her flattened ears and increased her speed. She faded into the darkness of the night and the Indian let her go.

He jumped from the pony to find Felipe in the grass. The boy looked up and their black eyes met for an instant.

"Well, I rode her and I said I would. She didn't fail me either."

These words were in Felipe's mind, though he had not the strength to utter them. He smiled at these last fleeting thoughts and then he died, the second man to do so who had coveted La Bruja.

Chapter 12

ONAK

I

The Indians did not forget La Bruja. They had as much admiration for a fleet-footed horse as had the gauchos and they were not so aware of her ugliness, concerned more by ability than beauty. The man who captured Felipe had also killed him and he had first claim to La Bruja because of this. When dawn came he set out in quest of her, knowing that she could not have traveled far. His two companions of the previous day joined in his search and they chose three wiry ponies from the herd, knowing that the chase might be a hard one.

Onak, like Felipe, had no doubts about catching La Bruja and even had he known that she had killed a man he would have felt no fear of her. Indian or gaucho, they shared the same skills and it never occurred to either that they could be defeated by a horse.

The three young warriors cantered steadily from the encampment, carrying with them spear and knife. Hunters and hunted, killers and killed, they knew the danger of traveling weaponless in this seemingly deserted and peaceful land. Relentless hatred existed between the gaucho and the Indian, even though their bloods were mingled. Behind every hill might lurk a

dozen soldiers from the outpost and, as the Indians had
taken Felipe unawares, so might they be taken.

Onak had little fear of soldiers, for their battles were
often half-hearted affairs. They hated the Indians, but
they hated their commanders more, and there were soldiers who deserted the fort and found shelter with the
Indians, preferring uncertain life among them to certain
death or long years of service in the army. But Onak
hated all the Christians and would rather kill them
than befriend them, even though they were outcasts
and lawless in their own society. This land was of his
people, from north to south, and the soldiers were of
the same blood as the Christian invaders who stole the
pampa, claimed the lakes and rivers and drove the
Indians away.

Today Onak did not think of soldiers. His tribe had
been peaceful for many months, attacking none but the
occasional lone traveler, so that the soldiers in the fort
knew not of their deaths. Onak thought only of La
Bruja and he searched for her with eager eyes, scan-
ning the hills and valleys new to her but known to him,
and the hoofs of all three ponies made no sound upon
the earth, for they slowed their pace to a walk, having
all day before them. The sun made long shadows of
them in the grass, but the rest of the land was shadowless, for there was not a cloud in the sky.

Suddenly one of Onak's companions halted. He took
Onak by the arm and pointed with his spear. He
pointed downward, for they were traversing a ridge of
land above a river and he had seen the mare below
them at the water's edge. She was unaware of them

above her as they sat their still ponies in silence, watching her.

They saw her drink her fill and shake her head when she was satisfied. She rubbed at the rope round her neck with a hind leg and chased several flies across her rump with snapping teeth. The sun glistened upon the shallow waters of the river and upon the blades of the three upright spears. It shone upon La Bruja's glossy back and upon the smooth skins of the Indians.

La Bruja was unaware of danger. There was the sound of water in her ears and the chirping of crickets in the grass, but the Indians were noiseless upon the hill-top and their ponies were silent too. She grazed beside the river in contentment, swishing her tail about her flanks as she pulled at the luscious grass, and she was lulled by the warmth of the sun and the pleasant sounds in her ears, forgetting the experience of the previous day because she was free again, Felipe did not follow her and she was unmolested.

The three Indians drew their ponies back from the ridge. La Bruja did not hear them, for their harness was nothing but halter and blanket and there were no metal bits to jingle as they moved their heads. Onak led his companions down the hillside and signaled that he should ride alone, encircling the right flank of the hill, while the others took the opposite direction. Thus they could come upon La Bruja from two sides and she would be trapped between them, for the river was in a valley with towering banks on either side.

They circled the base of the hill and the river was before them. Onak still held back until his two companions were in sight behind La Bruja and he waited

for them to set her galloping. While he waited he took
his lasso in his hands, holding the restless pony to
attention by the pressure of his knees, and a smile came
to his face while he waited, for soon La Bruja would
be his.

Suddenly the peace of the afternoon was disrupted.
His two companions rounded the far side of the hill at
a gallop, screeching as they had done the day before,
and they splashed across the river, waving their spears.
La Bruja flung up her head in alarm, grass still hanging from her jaws, but an instant was all she needed to
judge her enemies and the chase was on.

She followed the river which led to the flat pampa,
far ahead, meandering lazily between the hills which
sloped away to nothing in the distance. She galloped
with strength and power, refreshed by a morning of
relaxation, and the distance between her and the Indians steadily widened, for their ponies were not fleet
enough to keep apace with her.

Onak watched and waited and judged the distance
carefully. The cries of the Indians and the galloping
hoofs were a torment to his restless pony, so that when
the moment came and Onak gave him his head he flung
himself full pelt across the river in front of the frightened mare.

La Bruja saw this second trap and she whirled
swiftly back upon her tracks. But the other two were
still behind her and drawing closer while she faltered,
and for a moment she was confounded, not knowing
what to do. She reared and circled and hesitated, then
suddenly made up her mind, taking the only course
open to her, the hillside.

She tried to gallop up the slope, but it was too steep and uneven, slowing her to a steady but hasty climbing pace. She stumbled several times, unused to this kind of terrain, and fear almost drove her to panic as she clambered upward, for the ground was uncertain beneath her hoofs and slippery. Her two followers came behind her, urging their ponies faster than she could climb, but Onak took a different route. He knew of an easier trail which led to the hilltop and raced his pony toward it, hoping to make the ascent before La Bruja.

La Bruja halted several times. On the slippery and crumbling hillside she was in a trap of her own making and more than once she tried to take a downward course, distressed by two opposing fears. But the Indians behind her kept her to an upward climb and eventually she reached the top ahead of them. On solid, level ground she regained her confidence and hesitated no longer. Onak was nowhere in sight and she fled swiftly from her pursuers, far ahead of them once more.

Onak had tarried too long in making his ascent and he put aside his lasso to join his two companions in the chase, taking the boleadoras in his hand, for they could fly ahead of him with more accuracy than any lasso.

La Bruja led them far from the river. Now that she was running freely, panic left her and she flung out her legs to their full extent, covering more ground with a single stride than any of the Indian ponies could. She gained her second wind and her speed increased, and Onak cried out with despair as he saw her race ahead and felt his own mount tiring.

The chase continued throughout the afternoon. The

Indian ponies had great endurance and strong hearts, but they had not the speed to compare with La Bruja and their riders urged them in vain. La Bruja wearied too, but the memory of past experiences kept her long legs functioning until she knew she had shaken off her pursuers. A tide of white sweat coated her neck and flanks, her breath rasped through her open jaws, but when she finally allowed herself to halt the Indians were no longer following her.

She stood with heaving flanks and trembling legs, watching them as they rode back the way they had come, and a sense of triumph came to her panting heart as she watched them. Fear faded, her lungs expanded with less pain, and after a while La Bruja dropped her head to graze again. She was thirsty, but she remembered how she had been trapped between the hills beside the river and she suffered her thirst until she could find a new place to drink, too wary to go to the river again.

The sun completed its circle in the sky and darkness came to the land once more as it vanished behind a range of hills. La Bruja stood with pricked ears and distended nostrils, listening and breathing in the wind, for still she felt no security. Apart from the scuffling creatures in the grass she could hear no sound of danger and the smell of man was not in the air.

She lowered herself to the ground and was glad to ease her tired legs, blowing through her nostrils as if sighing with relief. Still she was watchful. Not until all anxiety faded did she finally succumb to sleep and even while she slept the muscles of her weary legs twitched spasmodically and her ears remained alert.

II

Onak had a new idea. He coveted La Bruja with as much desire as had Gregorio and Felipe, especially now that he had truly tested her speed and endurance, and even while riding his exhausted mount back to the encampment his mind was searching for another way to capture her. He could think of only one sure way, and, while La Bruja slept, he and four companions cantered silently across the pampa, each leading a second horse.

Where Onak had given up the chase, one of the Indians detached himself from the party and remained there. The others went ahead and at a certain distance a second Indian dropped out. So they continued until all four Indians with their ponies had stationed themselves as Onak suggested, for his plan was to make a relay of the chase so that when one pony tired another could take over. Onak would ride a fresh pony all the time, while La Bruja must run until exhaustion overcame her. With a plan like this he knew he could not fail and he awaited the coming of the new dawn with impatience, eager to find La Bruja once again.

The sun came and the sky seemed to be a reflection of a distant land with sea, black rocks and golden sands, all a pattern of the sun-touched clouds. Birds thrilled to the new day's dawning and their breasts swelled with song. La Bruja scrambled to all-fours and leisurely stretched herself, refreshed by sleep and hungry. Cautious habit made her look about first and test the early breezes, but the pampa seemed deserted and she dropped her head to graze.

Within a moment, however, her head was lifted, her ears taut, her body quivering, for she had felt a slight trembling of the ground and was alerted. The trembling became a definite, distant sound and La Bruja circled anxiously, staring in every direction, for she knew what the sound portended and was prepared for flight.

Suddenly she saw the approaching man on horseback. He was no more than a black smudge among the greenness, but La Bruja knew well that sign by now. There was no animal that moved so swiftly and appeared thus.

Still she hesitated, deciding upon the direction of her flight. To the west of her was the river and to the northeast of her the enemy. She turned southward and once again the chase was on. Fear was not within her yet. She still remembered her success of the day before and she was fresh, though hungry. The Indian who had put her to flight remained far distant, for Onak waited ahead of her, to the south.

La Bruja did not see him until she had passed him by, for he was well to the east of her and not conspicuous. Only when she had passed him did she become aware of the new man far closer in pursuit and she spurted ahead with fresh effort, struck by her first chill of fear.

Onak had guessed fairly accurately the direction she would take with a little persuasion and the first waiting horse was within a few miles of the trail she followed. La Bruja saw the stationary Indian with the ponies, but he was too distant to cause her to swerve away and change her route. The sight of him only made her increase her speed.

Onak lost ground changing ponies, but this caused him no worry, for the chase would be a long one and La Bruja would tire before the final horse was needed. He followed her with confidence and with pleasure, admiring her courage and endurance, for the sun was hot and the race unending.

The sun's position slowly changed. The hours passed and La Bruja's strength began to fail her. She put all her heart and power into her pounding hoofs and fear gave her added speed when weariness overcame her.

As time went by, and the Indian kept to her trail, La Bruja felt instinctively that she was doomed. She gave herself recklessly to the chase and the hot sun drew upon her strength, as did hunger, thirst and weariness. Her vision was blurred as she automatically moved her stiffening legs, her jaws fell open and she could not close them. She lost all sense of direction and speed, aware only of the steady hoofs behind her which threatened to overtake her.

Panic filled her. She did not even know that her pace was slowing, trying as she was to find new strength, and soon Onak was near enough to whirl her bole-adoras after her and be sure of success.

This he did. La Bruja heard them swish through the air and well she knew that sound by now. Her reaction was to leap forward, kicking out her hind legs in an effort to avert them, but she leaped too late and within a second, she was sprawling to the ground, landing heavily upon her flank, every part of her body jarred by the sudden impact.

She did not struggle up again, but lay where she had fallen, heaving desperately, almost choking in her breathlessness. She closed her eyes against the harsh glare of the brazen sun and when she had regained her breath her head fell back into the grass, for she had not the strength to rise.

Onak drew his pony close and dismounted. He held a lasso in his hands and this he put about her head without struggle on her part, shaping it in halter fashion. La Bruja shuddered at the human touch, but so exhausted was she that she could do nothing but accept him. She trembled violently, not only because her overstrained nerves reacted thus but because she knew what she must endure while in the power of this man. She waited to feel his angry kicks and thorny spurs, remembering Gregorio, but nothing happened.

Onak stood and watched her while she panted in the grass and he held the lasso slackly in his hand, knowing that she was incapable of escaping him. He made no sound while he watched her, but listened keenly to her heavy breathing, gladly noting that it became more normal as the minutes passed and that the rasping died away. At first he feared that she had strained herself too much, so gallantly had she tried to elude him, but she had the iron heart of her Criollo sire and suffered no inward damage.

For a long time Onak waited patiently beside La Bruja. Now and then he passed his hand across her outstretched body, pride of ownership overwhelming him when he thought of the treasure he had gained. Not only was she the swiftest horse he had ever seen but also one of the strongest. He would tame her and ride her into battle, for she was truly a warrior's mount, and in times of peace she would breed him colts, strong and swift, for his sons.

So Onak planned the future for La Bruja as she lay inert beside him in the pampa grass and he saw no ugliness in her lanky frame, only a swallow swiftness which one day he would share.

Chapter 13

INDIAN MASTER

I

The Indian, for all his lack of feeling toward his fellow men, showed great consideration toward his horse. Onak treated his wife little better than a slave, but La Bruja was the treasure of his life and he handled her with tenderness, an attribute of man that she had not yet experienced. Every day anticipating the brutalities she had suffered with Gregorio, La Bruja could not comprehend that this new master did not mean to harm her.

Onak weighted the lasso with a heavy log and left her to her own devices for many hours of the day, knowing that she could not escape him and prepared to use much patience in order to tame her. She dwelt, a prisoner, in this solitary fashion without the confines of the encampment in a deserted valley not far from the river.

This was a new experience for La Bruja. She was a captive and yet she had comparative freedom, able to move about at will within the scope of the long lasso. She was a prisoner of man and yet she saw him so rarely that at times she forgot that he existed. He came but once a day to see her and when he came he stayed for several hours, watching her but never touching her.

Onak had seen the uneven scars upon La Bruja's

flanks and he knew that she had been a captive once before and badly treated. He knew by her wild struggles, when first she regained strength enough to fight him, that she held great hatred toward mankind, for she lunged at him with snapping jaws and flailing hoofs, the urge to kill again within her. He saw her white-ringed, vicious eyes and flattened ears and all these things were signs of nurtured hatred, feelings not new within her. He knew that before he could hope to tame her he must undo the harm that another had inflicted and therefore he left her in peace until her hatred for him faded.

For three days La Bruja was alone. In the early hours of the first day she fought against the rope which held her, hating the feel of it about her head and ears, having known only the rope about her neck before. She learned, however, that the halter could not be discarded and she accepted it eventually because she had no other choice.

All that first day she was filled with fear and fury. She attacked the log to which the rope was tied and bruised her hoofs without destroying it. She reared and snorted and rolled her eyes in angry frustration, but there was nothing on which she could vent her anger. Eventually her fury died and she fell to grazing, ripping the grass with hasty bites, constantly alert, fear within her still.

The silence of the night, broken only by sounds she knew and did not fear, did much to pacify her anxious, angry heart. She examined every morning breeze and pricked her flattened ears, listening for danger, but there was neither scent nor sound to disturb her all the day. She grazed to satisfaction and basked in the warm sunlight and that night she stretched herself upon the ground so that her weary legs might rest.

The third day passed in a similar fashion and if the halter had not been about her head, nor the log existed to which it was tied, La Bruja would have forgotten that she was a prisoner.

The fourth day came and with it came the Indian. He halted his pony at some distance from La Bruja and dismounted, not venturing to approach her, for at the sight of him all her fury and fear returned.

She tried to flee, but the heavy log dragged against her head and held her back. She reared and pranced toward the Indian with striking hoofs, but again the log defeated her. She tried again to flee, she made a second attack. She grew savage with panic and anger, as all her efforts failed, and at last she stood and trembled, knowing that she could neither escape nor kill him.

All this while Onak did nothing. He watched La Bruja's struggles motionless and silent, and when she was still he advanced slowly toward her. In one hand he carried a large, earthenware bowl, in the other a skin fashioned to contain water. La Bruja watched him coming, but did nothing, waiting for him to make the first move, nervous and more afraid of him because he did not harm her. She saw him place the bowl firmly in the grass and pour water from the skin container into it. Then he backed away and she did not know whether to watch the bowl or the Indian, suspicious and afraid of both.

Onak remounted his pony and rode away. He did not look back, but slowly ascended the hillside out of the valley and disappeared from sight.

Long after he had gone La Bruja ventured forward to sniff and touch the bowl. She recognized the Indian's scent and drew back with nostrils wrinkling in disgust, fearing some trap. Nothing happened and the scent of the waiting water became a tantalizing presence near, for she had drunk no water in all these days. She grazed all round the bowl without touching it, but by the afternoon the Indian scent lingered only vaguely and her thirst was great. Gingerly she dipped her muzzle into the warm, still water and she forgot the man, her fear and her captivity. The water was good and she was thirsty.

After this Onak came every day to bring her water. La Bruja no more tried to attack him. Instead she stood her ground while he approached, body taut and trembling, ears flattened so that she looked even uglier in her fear. She saw that he performed the same actions every day, pouring water into the bowl, then backing slowly away, but each day he lingered longer in her presence until he saw her drink the water and ignore him.

When she did this Onak knew that La Bruja was losing her mistrust of him. He rejoiced to himself, for he was longing to ride her, longing to urge that powerful body to incredible swiftness, but, unlike Gregorio, his patience did not fail him and he judged La Bruja well, sensing when she was prepared to accept him and not touching her until then.

This day came very slowly, when the spring days were losing their cool freshness, lengthening to the sultry heat of summer. La Bruja was for long a prisoner in the valley and the earth about her was almost bereft of grass, for she ate in a steady circle and crushed the grass she did not eat beneath her ever-moving hoofs. Onak knew that he must move her, but still he hesitated, fearing to touch her too soon. He had spoken to her gently, using sounds rather than words, and some of the sounds he used were those he had learned from the foals in the herd, so that La Bruja twitched her ears and turned less vicious eyes toward him.

La Bruja could not comprehend this man and because of this she mistrusted him long after fear had faded. He no longer stood and watched her, but moved from side to side, drawing closer, uttering sounds as he came. Some she knew and some she had never heard before. When he made the sound of a hungry foal a vague memory within her was stirred, and to hear this sound from him confused her more. Instinct made her yearn toward the hungry foal, but knowledge made her see the man from whom the sound came and she was disturbed by such confliction.

Onak waited. Better that the mare should feel hunger than that she should lose her growing trust of him. He sensed her conflict and knew that his patience would be rewarded, for she was no longer ill-disposed toward him, accepting his presence calmly and often with curiosity. She pricked her ears and returned his steady gaze and for the first time she began to realize that man need not be an enemy.

II

La Bruja accepted Onak.

One morning when he came to her he did not only talk and move about her. He put out his hand and held it beneath her nose and in his palm was crushed a mouthful of grain for La Bruja, something she had neither smelled nor tasted before. She sniffed the proffering with care, hardly aware of the hand that held it, for the scent of the Indian was no longer strange to her, and, deciding that it was good to eat, she suddenly snaffled it up between her soft, pink lips.

Then Onak put out his other hand gently touched her head. She flattened her ears for a moment, then pricked them again, but she did not draw back. His hand was light upon her, not threatening or powerful.

She stood still while Onak gradually smoothed his hands over all parts of her neck and back and even when he stroked her belly and legs she was not afraid or startled. While he stroked her Onak uttered soft, encouraging sounds and La Bruja listened with one ear pressed back, liking the noises he made.

Then Onak sprang suddenly but lightly upon her back. La Bruja tossed her head and snorted with surprise, but the legs of the Indian hung loosely on either side of her, hardly touching her sensitive flanks, so that, although she trembled and was uncertain, she was still confident enough to accept him. Onak sat and stroked her neck, still talking to her in his own peculiar way, and though La Bruja had flattened her ears and rolled her white-rimmed eyes, she gradually relaxed to hear

his steady voice. After a while his weight did not per-
turb her.

Thus La Bruja accepted the domination of man. Onak
was clever, gaining her trust before attempting to command her, and she never felt whip or spur or heard an
angry voice while the Indian was her master. True, he
sometimes ran her almost to the point of exhaustion,
but she had treated herself thus and did not hate or
fear him for it. She never knew a bit between her
teeth, for the Indian guided her by his voice and knees
or by the reins he held, and she needed no encouragement when called upon to race.

Onak took La Bruja to the encampment. He haltered
her to a stake outside his toldo, the Indian's tent of
skins, and this was her home throughout the summer.
When the Indian was in the camp he did not let La
Bruja loose among the other ponies to graze and while
away the hours among her kind, but kept her near him,
for in his own way he loved her. The first thing he
did when he took her to the camp was to draw out his
knife and sever the old lasso about her neck. For a
long time afterward La Bruja felt strange without it.
She shook her head and stretched her neck, not understanding why the rope she had carried for so long
did not dangle in front of her legs. She was glad to
lose it, even though a second halter now kept her a
prisoner.

Haltered outside her master's toldo, La Bruja grew
bored and fretful. She had learned that it was useless
to try to escape the halter about her head, but still she
tossed and pulled and shook herself in vain. She
stamped her hoofs and snorted with impatience, and

the sweltering sun shone down upon her endlessly, for the shadow of the toldo was never long enough to include the spot where she was tethered. In the afternoons she dozed, resting all her weight on one side, eyes closed, tail automatically swishing as constant, buzzing, biting insects tormented her. They crawled about her eyes and up and down her legs. She twitched her skin spasmodically where her tail could not reach, but the flies only circled and returned once more to bother her until eventually she did not heed them.

The ground where she stood was grassless, the earth hardened and cracked by constant sun and lack of rain. Therefore she had nothing to nibble, nothing to do, and her restless heart grew heavy because of her enforced idleness. Even though she had accepted Onak, and did not resent him riding her, she was still wild in spirit, shying and trembling at the slightest unusual thing, afraid of any stranger. The wind called to her, the smell of the distant pampa, the singing birds; all reminded her of the life she had lost and made her fretful.

Onak would take her to graze and drink, and while she filled her belly, cropping the dwindling summer grass with hunger, he would sit astride her and talk to her, so that for a while she would forget her longing for freedom, listening to his voice and liking it.

But there were days when Onak and his friends set out early from the encampment, perhaps hunting meat, sometimes hunting men. Then La Bruja could fling out her eager, impatient legs, stretch her neck and race all the pent-up excitement out of her. The ground beneath her hoofs was hard, trembling as she pounded across it, and the cries of the whooping Indians filled her with a chill of fear and urged her faster.

There were many days when she galloped thus, until her flanks and neck were lathered and she gasped for breath, and because of these times she was able to bear the confinement of the encampment when there was nothing to do but stand and wait.

Onak was envied by his friends. He proved La Bruja's prowess time and time again, racing her against any and every horse the Indians possessed. She was fleeter than them all and possessed their staying power too so that no man could say, "She may be fast but mine is stronger."

Onak was proud of La Bruja. He not only wanted her fast but sure-footed too and he set about training her legs, the risk of injuring her one he had to accept.

He forced her to race full pelt down steep and slippery hillsides, he made her swim the river again and again. He ran her on soft, boggy ground and on one occasion made a long trek to the foothills of the mountains in the west, searching rocky ground over which he could race her too. He taught her to accept him in every position, whether he clung beneath her head with only one leg astride her or even if he twisted below her belly, teaching her to be his shield in times of battle. Her hardy legs accepted everything and soon she was able to take hills and rivers, hard ground and soft, with scarcely a falter in her stride, a perfectly trained Indian mount.

Onak ordered his wife to weave a special blanket for La Bruja, with wool dyed like the color of the sky, and he stroked her and talked to her and breathed gently

Onak knew that La Bruja was losing her mistrust of him.

in her nostrils, knowing that horses communicate with one another in this way.

La Bruja learned much about the humans among whom she dwelt. She saw the wife of Onak and his children, three young boys who toddled and fell and hurt themselves but rarely cried. She watched the woman as she cooked and wove and went about her many daily tasks. The Indians had settled in this part, although the white man had forbidden them the land, and they grew crops on the hillsides, which Onak's wife must tend with the wives of others, living unmolested while the commanders of the distant fort did not know that they were there.

La Bruja feared the little children, for they shouted and were rough, but she felt nothing for the woman who came not near her. She was employed continously with this and that, often within sight of La Bruja, always within her hearing, unless she was in the fields. The woman rarely spoke, unless it was to give a command to one of the children, and La Bruja accepted and soon ignored her presence, as did her master.

But although she tolerated the children, ignored the woman and accepted Onak without question, La Bruja could not endure the nearness of any other man. When the friends of Onak touched her, wanting to feel the strength of her legs, she would rear and shy and bare her teeth until Onak made them back away. Instinctively her fear and hatred toward mankind had not died, so deeply had it once been impressed upon her. Onak had overcome it with his patience and him she recognized as intending her no harm. All the rest she feared, remembering Gregorio, and she would not have them near her.

Onak did not look upon this as a fault. In fact it made him glad to see her thus, for she was truly his mount and no other man could ride her. There was arrogance in his flat, Mongolian face as he forbade another man to touch her and made his children keep away, and when he rode La Bruja he rode her with great pride.

Chapter 14

SURPRISE ATTACK

I

Summer passed away. Rain came in heavy storms and the hard, sun-parched land grew soggy and ran with water. The wilting grass struggled anew for life and a greenness came to it as the thirsty earth sucked in the water, giving fresh sap to all the many roots it nurtured. The sun grew temperate in its warmth and there were days of dullness when it had too little energy to pierce the grayness of the clouds.

In the southern land autumn came more quickly. Chill winds blustered in the valleys and swept over the hills. In the Indian encampment women searched the toldos for tears in the hides and set about repairing those they found before winter came upon them. They harvested the maize crops and stored grain where they could. They prepared for the long, cold months in many ways while the men did nothing but race and train their ponies, hunt for meat and kill the occasional traveler who ventured unwittingly across their chosen domain.

Few travelers had reason for coming so far south, especially in the worsening weather, and they afforded the savage Indians little sport. Onak, because of La Bruja, was more successful than most, for she could outrace the fastest fleeing horse, as several luckless travelers discovered. But Onak, in his eagerness to kill the men he hated, brought one too many to the ground.

While grazing La Bruja beside the river one afternoon, talking to her and stroking the thickening hair of her coat, he spied a man on horseback wading through the water lower down, obviously unaware of the Indian so nearby. By his shabby blue uniform and dangling sword, Onak knew him for a soldier, and with a grunt of pleasure he pulled La Bruja from her grazing and set her at a gallop after him.

The soldier heard his savage cry. It woke him from the reverie in which he had been riding all the afternoon and there was fear in his eyes as he lashed his horse with his whip and dug in his spurs, racing in vain against the swift La Bruja. He knew the Indian would overtake him and, in desperation, changed his tactics, abruptly spinning his horse round and charging upon the Indian, sword in hand. Deliberately he drew in close so that Onak could not throw his spear effectively and the two horses almost collided as they raced in opposite directions.

Onak could not turn La Bruja. The sword slashed down upon him, slicing his thigh as he swung sideways to avert it, but, even as blood spurted from the wound, he flung himself upon the soldier with a cry of mingled rage and pain.

They fell together to the ground, each struggling desperately to gain the upper hand, both men reaching for the knives at their backs, for the soldier had lost his sword and Onak his spear. Onak had the advantage, for the soldier was beneath him as they fell and, although his thigh was severed almost to the bone, he found strength enough to hold the other down and kill him.

He staggered back from the dead man, triumphant even in his pain, and he took the soldier's knife and sword and cap, then looked about for La Bruja. She had returned to grazing, not far from where the battle had been fought, and the soldier's gray gelding grazed beside her, unaware of the fate of his master.

Onak limped to La Bruja and now that the flush of victory had faded he felt the pain of his injured leg, gritting his teeth because he could hardly bear it. Somehow he managed to mount and take the other horse in hand. All the way back to the encampment he fought against failing consciousness and La Bruja's flank was stained with blood which left a trail in the grass as it dripped to the ground.

She took him faithfully to his toldo, knowing that something was amiss, for he lurched often and clung to her mane, and although she had killed Gregorio she was gentle with him because he had been good to her. As she neared the encampment other Indians saw her approach and came to help her injured master. La Bruja resented their nearness and their outstretched hands and Onak gasped for them to leave her, that she would take him safely home. They followed behind and when La Bruja halted at the toldo Onak found strength enough to tie her to the stake and caress her as usual before he left her, supported by other's arms. She never saw him again.

II

The soldier whom Onak had killed was an army scout. The commander of the outpost, some hundred miles distant from where the Indians were encamped, was suspicious of the lull in hostilities and vaguely disturbed by the occasional report of a missing man, known to be traveling that way. Therefore he sent out four scouts, giving them orders to return within a week and report as to whether they had seen anything suspicious.

Onak's soldier was not a good scout. He was young and he hated the life of the fort, so that when he was released for a week he spent the time wandering about the countryside, doing nothing in particular but enjoying his unexpected freedom.

The other scouts returned and all their reports were in the negative. They had traveled to the north, east and west and the commander waited impatiently for a report on the southern districts, where trouble was most likely. None came. Each day passed until the scout was long overdue and the commander guessed that he had either died or deserted. Either way a search for him must be made and when another week had passed the fort was spurred to activity by the early bugler calling them to horse. Some came grumbling, some came excited, some were afraid.

"The Indians have broken loose again," was the general refrain, and a shabby troop of men cantered through the open gates of the fort, hurrying southward, with orders to rout the Indians from their homes and

drive them farther away. More scouts were sent ahead
and when they met up with the column again they
returned with news of the encampment half a day's
ride distant.

Dusk was draping its mantle over the hills and valleys
as the small troop of soldiers reached the river, and
there they halted at the captain's orders, dismounting
in order to let their horses rest. Within ten miles the
Indian encampment lay and the soldiers were forbidden
to speak for fear that their voices would be overheard
by any wandering Indian who might chance to pass
that way.

The captain gave his men an hour's rest. Stars were
glittering in the sky and the moon glowed through a
haze of yellow-tinged clouds, illuminating but little the
hilly ground which lay between the river and the Indian encampment. The captain's plan was one of surprise attack. The Indians, unprepared for battle, would
be unable to retaliate effectively and casualties among
the soldiers would not be heavy.

Almost in silence, the gaucho soldiers remounted.
Bits jingled as horses shook their heads, but the tread
of many hoofs upon the soft earth of the river's bank
was only slight and it was an ominous group of men
that came suddenly upon the encampment, hardly
guarded by watchmen.

The encampment was in a narrow valley, with low,
cultivated slopes to the west of it and steep hills on the
eastern side, which spread like an undulating plateau
to overlook the river from whence the soldiers came.
The hills threw a dark shadow across the ragged
collection of toldos, but two brightly burning fires

glowed through the gloom so that the position of the camp was plain to see by the soldiers approaching silently from the east.

Dogs gave the alarm. A lone wanderer on the outskirts of the camp heard the gentle hoofs and set up an urgent barking, to be chorused by every dog that scrounged about the toldos, searching for offal. The Indians were warned, but the warning came too late. Even as they ran for their horses, spears in hand, the troop of soldiers swept at a gallop down the hillside, swords raised aloft and glinting as they neared the flaring fires, prepared to destroy everything in their path.

Women and children rushed out of their toldos, hearing the trampling hoofs all about them and the clash of sword against spear. Horses whinnied shrilly, men yelled and cursed in fury, and the skinny dogs raced to and fro, barking and yelping with excitement. In the darkness, with only firelight to guide them, confusion reigned. Riderless horses plunged among fighting men and blundered into toldos. The soldiers hacked and slashed at everything they could find and one by one the toldos collapsed, many of them giving way under the weight of trampling horses.

Soon groans of pain joined the chorus of noise, together with wild shrieks as bewildered women ran to protect children cowering under a soldier's threatening sword. There was no compassion in any heart that night. The soldiers had come to kill and they did their duty recklessly, felling babes and old women as well as warriors. Orders were shouted but remained unheard and soon flames flickered among the fallen toldos, catching hold slowly at first but stirred to strength by the conquering soldiers.

La Bruja, still tethered outside her master's toldo, was filled with growing fear, not understanding the meaning of all the noise and fire and galloping horses. She tossed her head and grew in restlessness, flattening her ears and rolling her eyes as memories were stirred within her.

The toldo in which Onak lived was on the western outskirts of the encampment and, as yet, the soldiers had not ventured so far, attacking centrally where the most damage could be done. But soon fear-stricken women began running that way, dragging children behind them, searching for safety they knew not where, but realizing they must escape the village or die. Soldiers chased after them and cut them down and one man, seeing La Bruja tied where she was, cut her loose with a slash of his sword. His rearing horse pawed against the sides of the toldo and soon it collapsed, smothering Onak as he lay helpless and silent.

La Bruja, finding herself so suddenly free, whirled away from the village and galloped with flattened ears into the darkness. Fear drove her and she fled without knowing where she went, taking hills and valleys in her stride without faltering, as Onak had taught her. She raced with the cries and groans of the Indians still in her ears and the sky was red behind her as flames leaped upward, destroying all that the soldiers could not destroy.

For a long time she ran, pursued by fear if not by man, and not until she was aware only of the noise of her own hoofs did she shorten her stride. She cantered a little way further until she was sure of the silence, and then she halted, turning to stare behind her. She saw only a vague red glow over the hills, which might have been the sun fading into the blackness of night except that the glow was in the north and not in the west. She was too far away now for sounds to follow her, but it was only slowly that her fear faded, for the terror she had left behind her was difficult to forget.

Chapter 15

THE LIFE OF THE HERD

I

The smoke-gray stallion paused in his grazing and raised his head. His tiny ears flicked rapidly back and forth, his black nostrils suddenly distended, and an eagerness seemed to fill him as he stood for several minutes in this manner, quivering although he did not move. He was a small animal and age had taken away the handsomeness which in his youth he had possessed. His strong, well-muscled body was battle-scarred, marked in deep clefts where vicious hoofs had struck him, and the little ears were chewed and pointless. But he held his head proudly, arrogance in his roman profile, and his long black tail rippled like a banner as he stood smelling and listening on the hillside.

Below him, in a small semi-arid valley, grazed his mares, more than forty of them. They wandered back and forth, unheedful of his presence above them, bodies slack, heads drooping as they pulled at the scrubby grass. Only the foals were lively, dancing and fighting together, dashing back and forth, raising clouds of dust as they did so.

At the moment the stallion was not interested in his mares. He had caught a new scent and it was this that held his attention. As if suddenly deciding what to do, he climbed to the summit of the hill upon which he grazed, halting again at its crest, commanding from this point a wide view of the surrounding countryside.

In the distance were mountains with solid dark bases, but with peaks lost in an almost constant shroud of mist. The sky above them was white, becoming blue as it arched over the stallion's head, and between the mountains and the hill on which he stood lay an area of undulating scrubland, with long stretches of infertile earth forming barren hillsides and uninviting valleys.

The wind blew against the stallion as he surveyed the silent land and his black, unruly mane was tugged in its wake, his forelock straining backward between his questing ears. Suddenly the stallion saw that which he was searching. Not far below him, coming nonchalantly round the base of a hill, was a solitary mare, and she wandered along in no special hurry, examining the ground with her nose, occasionally halting to nibble a mouthful of coarse grass as she came upon it. She was unaware of the watching stallion, unaware of him until his hoofs broke the silence as he raced down the hillside to greet her, head flung back, prancing with eager steps.

La Bruja shied away, startled. Her reaction to racing hoofs was always the same, for still she held an instinctive fear of recapture, even though she had wandered unmolested about the countryside for many months. She had not forgotten the men who had chased her and a thrill of fear welled within her until she saw that the stallion was riderless.

Fear died. The stallion slowed his pace and halted, tossing his heavy head up and down, grunting, nickering and snorting eagerly. He was smaller than La Bruja, much smaller, for she had grown a great deal in five years and stood almost sixteen hands high. Somehow his smallness seemed to be of no account, for he was masterful and confident, while La Bruja was shy.

It was a long time since La Bruja had known the company of her own kind. Ever since the skewbald stallion left her she had dwelt alone or in the company of man. She had forgotten the life of the herd, forgotten the call of one horse to another, and her life had been empty in all the long months after Onak had gone.

She had roamed southward again, leaving the pampa far behind her, coming to a land of bitter winter, making hoofprints in the snow as she struggled against swirling, icy winds. The snow melted and the ground was soggy beneath her hoofs until she came upon the hardness of rock which she had only once felt before. This was a strange land in which she wandered and, as the spring approached, she searched in vain for growing giant thistles and patches of clover, finding only clumps of wiry grass, unpalatable to her pampered tongue, until hunger drove her to take her fill of anything slightly eatable.

La Bruja did not like this new land. The winter was cruel and even the early spring days were harsh, with a glaring sun that gave no warmth and a hard ground that produced no sustenance. She learned to survive on what she could find and her flanks grew lean as her body adapted itself to a frugal diet. Her legs grew firmer and her hoofs more hard as she trod the rocky ground daily and the long hairs of winter did not fall with such rapidity this year, for spring was long in coming.

Springtime roused the same excitement in La Bruja as it had ever done, even though the countryside about her seemed little changed by the bright new season. Birds called and preened their plumage, but this was not the land for the summer visitors, so that the sky was rarely crowded by winging flocks returning.

La Bruja's feelings remained undefined. A vague restlessness within her made her gallop and kick and search the wind. These were the outward signs of the longing which always came to her when spring covered the land, a longing she never clearly understood.

Once she had searched a stallion. This time he had found her and La Bruja was not sure that she wanted him, trotting away, wheeling about, keeping him at bay with bucks and kicks which were half playful, half serious. The stallion followed her. He knew her game well and was prepared to let her have her way, trying to encourage her to friendliness at the same time with gentle whinnyings and snorts and occasional caresses with his head when she allowed him near enough.

La Bruja forgot any feelings of antagonism toward the small, smoke-colored stallion. Delight surged through her as the blue sky glowed with warmth upon her back and the stallion called to her. Her independence melted away, her desire for solitude was lost and she wanted only to draw her new companion closer, teasing him a little with pretended disdain, knowing full well that this would attract him more.

So La Bruja and the stallion played all morning and La Bruja was like a filly again in her joy, forgetting

everything in the pleasure of her new companion. At
first the stallion drew back from her when she rubbed
her head against him, for still she had the Indian
halter round her head and he was suspicious of it. It
did not smell of man, only of La Bruja, but somehow he sensed that it was something unnatural and
he grabbed it with his teeth, trying to pull it away. La
Bruja tossed her head and jumped backward, suddenly
fearful again, the stallion's action in that moment too
much like an action of man. Her eyes rolled, flashing
white, and the stallion took heed of her anger and
did not attempt to grab at the halter again.

Later on, when he had wandered far with La Bruja
from the hill on which he had been grazing, he remembered his mares in the valley and was suddenly afraid
for them. He had left them unprotected for many hours
and anxiety overwhelmed him as he realized that he
was far from them.

He startled La Bruja as his manner changed. From
a playful, caressing companion he became an angry
overlord, driving La Bruja before him against her will,
biting at her rump and withers if she tried to turn
away. He forced her at a gallop back to the valley of
his mares and when she saw them remembrance of her
old life flooded her. She resisted violently the stallion's
will. She would not live among his mares and she
swerved suddenly away, intending to escape.

The stallion would not let her. Each and every mare
he treasured and now he possessed La Bruja as well
as all the rest. He raced after her with a scream of
fury and La Bruja flattened her ears as she heard his
enraged cry, cringing beneath the punishing blows and

bites with which he inflicted her before finally throw-
ing himself against her with such force that she lost
balance and fell heavily to the ground.

The stallion had no mercy on her. He lashed her with
his hoofs as she rose again and sank his teeth into her
neck, so that, terrified, she obeyed him and fled toward his mares, finding peace among them as his whirlwind fury died and he let her alone.

For the rest of the day La Bruja was angry. She
watched the stallion and had no appetite to graze even
though the grass in the valley was good. She ignored
the friendly overtures of curious mares and snapped
angrily in self-defence at those antagonistic toward
her, but she knew that she could not escape her latest
captor, even though no rope held her. His quick bright
eyes were everywhere and even while he grazed La
Bruja knew that he was watching her.

With the fading of daylight La Bruja's anger died.
The silent valley was peaceful, as one by one the mares
awkwardly stretched themselves out upon the ground
to rest. The young colts flopped at all angles, safe in
the knowledge that their mothers guarded them, and
they were nothing more than black heaps upon the
ground, losing form in the creeping shadows. La Bruja
wandered back and forth among them, gazing at the
stallion now and again who had made his abode on the
hillside for the night, and soon a desire for sleep overcame her too.

She settled herself among the other mares, no longer
so completely desirous of solitude, and as the moon set
out upon its nightly ritual, silhouetting ragged clumps
of grass against the naked earth, La Bruja fell asleep.

II

The seasons passed away. La Bruja grew accustomed to the strangeness of the land in which she dwelt, accepting the lack of varied grazing and thriving well enough on what she could find. The summer heat was milder here and the winds almost invariably struck with a chill. There were no hot winds in this region and the not-far-distant mountains were streaked with snow, unchanging in their aspect from month to month until the winter came. Then the higher mountains were clad in a mantle of whiteness which sparkled diamond-like when the sun was strong, and La Bruja learned to paw at the snow which covered her part of the earth, finding the grass beneath it tasteless and soggy but necessary if she were to survive the winter.

Though forced to dwell among the mares, La Bruja kept herself as much apart from them as possible. She could not change her whole way of life so suddenly, and still she yearned for the singular life she had always led, discouraging friendly overtures with threatening teeth or a hind leg. The mares learned to be wary of her, and, although never hostile toward her, they ignored her, leaving her to graze and laze alone.

The stallion ignored her too. Now that he had won her she interested him no more than did the others. He guarded them all equally well, watching over them from a distance, rarely coming among them.

Often La Bruja was restless. There was nothing to fear here and she had forgotten many of her anxieties,

left in peace for so much time, but within her was the
knowledge of her other land, the place where grass was
plentiful and the sun pleasant, where even the air was
different. She hankered for her own country without
even understanding the cause of her restlessness, forgetting the fears which had driven her to seek new
pastures.

As the weeks and months passed uneventfully by, La
Bruja grew fat again, as, for the third time, she was
in foal. Even in her restlessness she knew contentment
and, although there were days when she eagerly
breathed in the northern winds with pricked ears and
trembling body, she was loath to do more than graze
and doze and find herself sheltered sleeping spots for
the night.

Summer, autumn and winter passed away and all
this time La Bruja dwelt with the herd into whose company she had been forced. She was no more friendly
with any of the mares, she had no more accepted a
communal life, and as the struggling spring warmth
overcame the lingering days of winter coldness, she
became more antisocial, seeking a solitary place
far from the mares, instinct once again assisting her,
for she had long since forgotten Thamár.

A suitable place for the birth of the foal was difficult to find. La Bruja searched vainly for something
more than rocks and scraggy bushes, turning away dis-
satisfied from every likely place, instinctively rejecting
them, although she was hardly aware of what she
searched. Here there were no tall thickets of grass, no
screens of giant thistles, no cane-brakes. Here there
was nothing but hard ground and La Bruja wandered

disconsolately from place to place until eventually necessity forced her to choose a spot behind a pile of rocks, far enough from the herd but unsheltered from the whims of the weather.

La Bruja's foal was born during a thunderstorm, tumbling to the rocky ground as lightning flashed and sheets of rain pounded earthward. A skinny, black colt, he nearly drowned in the miniature lake which had formed itself about La Bruja as she stood shivering in the concave patch of earth she had chosen.

The sky was black, though the afternoon was scarcely over, and La Bruja licked furiously at her second youngling, pushing him from the puddle in which he lay, flattening her ears against the cannon-like thunder. The colt's first sights and sounds and feelings were terrifying, but somehow he managed to ignore the tempest which beat against his frail young flesh, staggering upon his wobbly legs, flopping into the puddle again as he lost his balance, spluttering out mouthfuls of water and shaking his shaggy head.

He was a big colt, solid of bone and body, already thickly coated with silky hair. Its glossy blackness was marred by the mud which clung to his knobbly knees and flanks, but this was of no importance to him. He ignored the discomfort of a dripping, mud-streaked coat as much as he ignored the violence of the storm, and when he had learned to keep his balance he searched greedily for the milk of life, blundering and bleating, then sucking with joy.

The storm seemed everlasting. The heavens split open with gashes of blue-and-silver light and La Bruja bowed her head against the fury of the elements, able

to withstand it calmly only because of the foal. She let
the black colt drink his fill and while he sucked, the
rain beating down upon his eager body and her exhausted one, she forgot about the storm, completely
engrossed by her second youngling, feeling again all
she had felt for Thamár.

The angry sky grew calm again. Black clouds were
swept away by a freshening breeze and La Bruja
shivered with cold as the wind's callous fingers dug
into her soaking body. The colt shivered too and clung
close to her, pushing and prodding with his small,
blunt head, seeking the warmth which at the moment
she was unable to give him.

The sun began to shine, making silver pools of the
water captured everywhere in dents in the ground. The
scent of the rain-soaked earth was sharp with a tang
of vivacity and La Bruja grew glad as she breathed in
the clean, fresh air.

She looked about, searching for a place not wet
where she could lie with her foal and rest, but everywhere water clung to the earth. Eventually she chose
a place in the sunshine, wet but warm, and there she
basked until the daylight faded, the colt sleeping beside her, drawing breath in short, sharp snorts obliv-
ious of the world into which he had been born.

Chapter 16

RETURN TO THE PAMPA

I

As she had done before, La Bruja took advantage of
the stallion's relaxed vigilance over her to escape from
his herd.

Not only was she anxious to live alone again. With
the coming of the early spring days she had been
possessed by a desire to return to her own country,
longing for the grass and the softness of the pampa, unable to accept the harshness of the southern land. She
instinctively knew what direction she must take, heading northward feeling the winds that swept across the
pampa, breathing in with eagerness the scents carried
before them.

Gladly she began her northward trek. There was no
question of loneliness, for the black colt frolicked beside her all the way, halting only when he was hungry
or tired, and he seemed to have the strength and endurance of his dam, for each day they covered many
miles and the colt played as he traveled. Only in the
first few days did La Bruja travel fast, afraid that the
stallion might come in search of her, but then she relaxed her pace, hearing no hoofbeats behind her, catching no scent of him.

Still La Bruja wore the halter about her head. She
had long since forgotten Onak, even though she had

not forgotten her violent hatred of Gregorio. Onak's kindness had made less impression upon her than the brutality of the other.

She eventually came back to the river, passing the place where her Indian master had killed the soldier, but no memories stirred within her except the instinctive knowledge that the place was not new to her. It took her a long time to reach the river, for she had wandered far southward before meeting with the smoke-gray stallion and the fresh days of spring were already lengthening into the drier days of summer.

She lingered long beside the river, gorging herself with the sweet, thick grass which grew on its banks, and the colt raced back and forth while she ate, discovering his own image in the water with much surprise, paddling his small black hoofs, startled at the coldness and the strange substance of the water. He had inherited La Bruja's love of running and when his mother set off at an easy canter he flung himself after her with joy, galloping madly to keep apace with her, tossing his head with glistening eyes as the wind rushed past him, discovering the thrill of speed.

The colt grew quickly and as he grew La Bruja experienced again all the pleasures and anxieties she had known with Thamár. He was not as good-looking as her first youngling, lacking the slender build of the filly; heavier in the leg, thicker in the neck, blunter in the head. Even so, he was not ugly and his black coat shone with blueness beneath the glittering sunlight.

La Bruja's solitude was not to last. The colt was little more than a month old when a red roan stallion came prancing along the river valley, whistling through his

nostrils as he called to the mare, for it was the time of
marauding stallions. La Bruja heard but did not heed
his cry, breaking into a trot in the opposite direction,
nickering for the colt to follow her.

Her young black son ignored her. Filled with the
curiosity of youth, he stood staring at the approaching
stallion, seeing for the first time another of his kind. He
flicked his bushy tail delightedly, then pranced toward
the stallion, anxious to play, but the big horse ignored
him, intent upon La Bruja. The colt was not accustomed
to being ignored. La Bruja played with him whenever
he was near and he could not understand the stallion's
indifference. Again he approached the roan, circling
him at a frolicking canter, bucking and rearing, pawing
the air in mock anger as one day he might paw in
reality.

The roan was a bad-tempered creature, past his
prime, and he had lost the herd he once possessed to
a younger, stronger stallion. He saw the hesitant La
Bruja far ahead and was irritated by the colt which ran
about him, pestering him like a buzzing fly. Suddenly
he lunged with flattened ears and snapping teeth,
missing the colt by half an inch, and La Bruja, seeing
his action, gave out a shrill whinny of fear, calling her
disobedient son again.

Still the colt ignored her, not realizing that the
stallion's attack was not meant in play. How could he
realize it when he had never known anything but tenderness and pleasure? La Bruja, aware of his danger
and seeing that the colt would not obey her, turned
back to fetch him. She raced toward him, filled with

sudden fear, and the stallion went to meet her, forgetting the colt in his eagerness.

La Bruja did not want him. She wanted only to get her youngling safely away from his vicious hoofs and she shied away from him with flattened ears, anger rising above her fear. The black colt stood and watched them, his eager ears flicking back and forth, trembling with excitement. He saw his mother snap and kick and gallop away. He saw the stallion stamp and rear and chase after her and, thinking it a game they played, he gladly joined in the race, darting between them, circling first La Bruja and then the stallion.

Great was the rage of the stallion. He could not overcome La Bruja and he could not rid himself of the colt. He screamed wildly and stood on his hind legs, pawing the air, and as the colt came darting toward him again, lammed out with a heavy hoof and sent him sprawling to the ground.

The colt made no sound as he crumpled under the blow, but La Bruja uttered a wild cry as she saw it, a cry of mingled rage, fear and despair. She flung herself upon the stallion and in her heart was all the bitter hatred that had fired her to kill the gaucho and the puma. Her swift hoofs crashed down upon the stallion's back. She tore at him with furious teeth and the roan fell back under her blows, astonished by her savagery. Disconcerted, never before attacked by a mare, he fled, forgetting all his previous desires in bewilderment.

La Bruja did not follow him. Her tempestuous fury died and she turned in anxiety to her foal, who still lay where he had fallen. Fearfully, La Bruja nuzzled him, pushing him, trying to encourage him to rise as

Vicente told them his news and his plan for the horse hunt.

she had done when he first learned to use his sturdy legs. The colt was limp and heavy, but he did not smell of death, and so La Bruja stood and sniffed him over, trembling and grunting, occasionally pushing at him again, not understanding why he could not rise.

Great was her joy when the colt suddenly twitched and kicked out his legs. She began again to push and nuzzle him, grunting encouragingly as the little creature staggered weakly to all fours. The stallion's hoof had, luckily, only glanced upon the colt's skull, knocking him unconscious, making a deep gash behind the ear.

La Bruja found the wound and licked at it industriously, almost knocking her youngling to the ground again in her anxiety. For a long time it was red and raw and pestered by flies, and for a long time La Bruja daily cleansed it with her tongue, instinctively knowing what she must do.

For some time the colt was weak, without appetite, wanting only to lie down and sleep, and La Bruja was patient with him, ignoring the tantalizing winds that called her home. But after lingering many days in the same place the colt grew strong again and La Bruja suddenly left the river valley with him, climbing the hills she had climbed with Onak astride her, heading northward once more.

II

More than two years had passed since La Bruja left her own country, driven away by fear. More than two years since she had killed the gaucho. Two years since

Felipe had promised to capture her and ride her. But in that time she was not forgotten.

The barber in the town often spoke of La Bruja, telling his customers of the offer he had made to the young stranger in the pulpería, laughing as he always finished, "And still he hasn't come back for a shave."

The barber's interest was in Felipe, but his customers were nearly always more interested in the horse, often asking a second time for a description of her, and these men also called her La Bruja, for she was ugly and wicked, as all witches are reputed to be.

Naturally enough, the barber always exaggerated his story. No one really expected him to tell the exact truth and as time passed La Bruja became a fabulous creature in his imagination, huge and powerful, with a speed bordering on the mythical. As he emphasized her prowess, so he emphasized her brutality. Soon it was two or three men that she had killed instead of only one, and while the barber neatly passed his razor over rarely shaven faces he plunged into gory details of the state in which the several bodies were found, even suggesting, though not pressing the point, that La Bruja was carnivorous.

His tales fired the imagination of many a young adventure seeker and supplied food for thought to those who had not heard the story before. They could not pass it off as just a tale of the barber to while away the time and keep his clients interested. Other men verified the existence of La Bruja and there were many who had seen the body of Gregorio.

There was not a man who passed through the barber's hands who did not hear of La Bruja and eventu-

RETURN TO THE PAMPA

ally some of them began to wonder what had happened to Felipe, whether she had killed him too.

One man in particular was interested in her. He was called El Ciego because he was blind in one eye. A heavily built, aging fellow he was, and his profession was horsebreeding. He prided himself upon being the owner of every unusual horse the pampa had to offer and certainly his stock was large and strange. Richer than most of his associates, he lived in comfort on a rancho not far from the town and the pampa surrounding his home was grazed by horses of every conceivable color, many of which the gauchos had never before seen or imagined.

His pride were the eight palominos of his personal string, bred after many years of experiment, and he cared for them more than he cared for his children. He offered strings of albinos for sale, piebalds, skewbalds and apaloosas, but his prices were higher than the normal man could afford, so that no one could compete with him. Most people looked upon him as an eccentric and no doubt he was as far as horses were concerned.

When he heard of La Bruja he immediately wanted to own her, not that he thought much of her coloring when he asked for her description. But the tales filled him with anxiety to own her, for he was unable to hear of any unusual horse without wanting to possess it.

Rich enough to employ several gauchos to guard his horses, he ordered them to keep constant watch for La Bruja and let him know just as soon as she was sighted. Months passed by and no one ever saw her and sometimes El Ciego was moody with smouldering rage when he considered the possibility that Felipe might already own her. He told the barber that if Felipe ever came to town with the mare he must let him know, feeling sure that he could tempt the boy to exchange her for some other horse or horses. But Felipe never came and El Ciego grew more and more possessed by the idea of owning La Bruja, simply because he could not have her.

It came to be generally known that El Ciego wanted La Bruja and that he had offered either horses or money in exchange to any man who might catch her, adding to her value. There were many gauchos who looked out for her when they happened to ride that way or stopped to rest in the shadow of the ombú where La Bruja had killed, but the story was now a joke with them and they never expected to find her.

III

La Bruja returned to her old haunts in the autumn, when the fierce heat of summer had gone and the dying grass was newly revived by heavy showers. She was aware of great contentment when she trod her own land again, recognizing the lagoons which once she had frequented, where the last flocks of flamingoes prepared themselves for their long flight to the isles off the western coast, constantly following the sun. She was too late for juicy thistle leaves or even fallen seeds, but they would come in their season, for the land was never barren here.

More than a year had passed since she had been chased by man and La Bruja had forgotten all her fears, forgotten them as she had forgotten the halter round her head, her last remaining link with mankind. When she had left this land it was with Gregorio's lasso about her neck and now she returned with Onak's halter to mark her and make her conspicuous.

While she traveled northward, the black colt grew in size and strength and handsomeness. His legs, though thick, were long like La Bruja's and it seemed that he was to inherit her swiftness, for he galloped easily beside her now, his black muzzle touching La Bruja's flank, letting her know that he was beside her still and not lagging behind.

When they reached the pampa he was quick to appreciate the richness of the land, if only for its softness beneath his hoofs. There was a new thrill in racing with resilient earth beneath him and he tired less quickly in the grass. The grass became of interest to him, too, for he was nearing six months old and the milk of his mother no longer completely satisfied him.

While La Bruja grazed tranquilly, the colt examined the grass, sniffing at it and sniffing at his hoofs, nibbling at them both as if unable to distinguish the difference between them. He snorted and grunted and jumped with pretended surprise, but he learned that the grass was good to eat. Soon mother and son grazed side by side, though the colt still returned to La Bruja when he was tired, finding in her comfort as well as satisfaction.

Thus the days and weeks passed away and when winter came La Bruja felt no urge to travel even farther northward, glad to be back in the place where she was born, not feeling the sudden coldness, for she had endured far worse in the districts of the south. She saw herds of horses in the distance but kept apart from them, preferring her solitude, but she hardly watched the horizon now, having been lulled into a sense of security after living so long without fear.

Chapter 17

THE TRAP

I

Before the winter had passed La Bruja was spotted and chased once again. She was seen from a distance by a young gaucho who had passed through the town only a week earlier, hearing her story for the first time.

When he saw her grazing with the colt beside her, not aware that he was watching her, he hardly dared to believe that it might be La Bruja, thinking that perhaps the story had colored his reasoning. He tried to draw closer without attracting her attention, noticing that she was tall and dark as the barber had said, and when La Bruja was startled, jerking up her head suddenly at the sound of his horse, he saw how ugly she was.

With a whoop of delight he set his horse at a gallop after her, for she had fled with the colt at the first sight of him. Vainly he whipped and spurred his mount in pursuit, but the little horse was left far behind. The gaucho disconsolately drew him to a halt, although now his last remaining doubts were dispelled, for the mare fled as though she had wings and the colt hardly lagged behind her.

Vicente was looking for work, traveling toward an estancia some fifty miles distant in the hope that he might be employed there. Filled with excitement by the discovery of La Bruja, he changed his mind and turned his horse about, making for the town once again, intending to find the home of El Ciego, of whom the barber had spoken, and tell him the news.

By the time he reached the town he had changed his mind. He remembered El Ciego's offer of money or horses to the man who caught La Bruja and he realized that his information alone would be of little value, worth no more than a meal or perhaps the offer of a job. Therefore he decided to talk the matter over with a couple of friends he had made in the pulpería, thinking that if they caught La Bruja between them they would be able to demand whatever they wished of the horse-breeder.

His two new acquaintances were still in town. They too were without work and while they had money were in no hurry to leave. They spent most of their lives in the emptiness of the pampa and even a town so small, possessing nothing more than a few streets of houses, a church, the pulpería and the barber's parlor, made a change. When they had spent their money they would leave, glad enough to do so, for at heart they preferred the pampa. For the moment they were content to leave their horses grazing freely outside the town and to sit and talk in the pulpería, or perhaps hear of a dance to go to at a nearby rancho.

Vicente told them his news and his plan. They looked very much alike as they sat together in the obscurity of a flickering candle on a corner table. They were dressed in faded brown chiripá, a kind of trouser which was no more than a square of cloth wrapped round their waists and pulled up between their legs; striped ponchos, for it was cold; and roughly made boots. Even in appearance there was little to tell between them, for all three were swarthy-skinned, black-haired and young.

At first the others laughed to hear Vicente's words.

"I don't believe she even exists," said Miguel. "It's just a barber's tale."

"But I saw her," insisted Vicente. "I tried to catch her, but never for one moment could I draw near enough, and my horse is as fast as any."

"All right, let's go," said the other, Santiago by name. "It won't do any harm and I wouldn't mind having a couple more black horses. El Ciego can supply them for me if we catch her."

The three men set out on their quest the following morning and before them they drove their horses, well rested after their masters' sojourn in the town. Santiago had six black geldings, two bays and a gray bell-mare, while Miguel had five duns and four bays, including his mare. Vicente had only his one horse and he envied the others their troops, thinking that he would demand many horses of El Ciego and be as proud of them as were Miguel and Santiago.

He suddenly remembered La Bruja's colt, saying to Santiago, as he had a passion for blacks, a rare color among the Criollo ponies: "The mare has a black colt, too. Perhaps you'd like to have him when we capture her."

"If we capture her," the man replied. "Let's concentrate on doing that first. There's plenty of time for dreaming afterwards."

The three gauchos searched for ten days before finding La Bruja, and Vicente grew anxious for fear that she should have already escaped them. It was a gray, cold day when they saw her, grazing afar off, and they drew their mounts to a halt quietly, fearing to put her to flight before they could be ready to chase her.

Santiago and Miguel dismounted to hobble their bell-mares, knowing that they could safely leave their other horses without tethering them, for they would not stray far from the mares. When they had done this Santiago announced that he had a plan for capturing La Bruja.

"If she's even half as fast as the barber says she is we'll never catch her," he said, his black eyes sparkling with pleasure, for there was nothing any gaucho liked more than pitting his strength and wits against a horse.

"The best thing to do is get the colt first. If she's any sort of a mother she'll be distracted enough to forget us and then we'll have her."

The others agreed that this was a good idea and they chose their three best horses, lending one to Vicente for the occasion, as his mount was tired, taking their boleadoras in hand as they mounted, feeling sure of success.

II

La Bruja was unaware of the approach of the three gauchos until they were fairly close. The wind was not in her favor, so that even the tinkling bells of the gauchos' mares were not heard by her. The colt saw them first and La Bruja was warned by him, even though he knew no sense of danger.

He lifted his head from grazing and saw the distant riders, staring at them with frank curiosity, ears pricked, nose quivering, eyes glistening. La Bruja saw his attitude and followed his eager gaze, uttering a snort of dismay and sudden fear as she pushed her son before her and broke into a gallop. The colt caught her fear, suddenly remembering the last time they had been chased, and he fled with flattened ears, listening for his dam as she came behind him.

They could not shake off the gauchos. La Bruja, in fear, stretched herself to a faster pace and as she did so the colt fell back, running madly behind her but losing ground every moment. La Bruja turned and called him, urging him to try harder, and then she raced on, eyes wild with terror, fearing for her colt as much as she feared for herself.

It began to rain. The sky grew black as if in fury at what it witnessed and a sudden cloudburst unleashed a heavy torrent upon the horses and the men. To La Bruja the rain meant nothing. She ran swiftly and confidently, though it streamed over her flanks, but the colt was disconcerted as it flooded his eyes and beat upon him. He gasped and snorted and shook his head and this small action was enough to make him lose more ground.

He saw his mother far ahead and had not the breath to call out to her and she, confident of her power to escape her pursuers, forgot that her colt could not run so fast and left him far behind.

The gauchos came on with loud yells, cracking the air with their flat whips, but there was always too much distance between them and La Bruja for an effective throw of the boleadoras. It seemed that she ran with wings, her hoofs hardly touching the ground, but the colt was exhausted and ran with leaden hoofs until he could run no more.

He halted suddenly, turning to watch the approaching gauchos, gazing after his distant mother, panting with heaving flanks, crushed by the heavy rain as well as by breathlessness. The gauchos did not even need to rope him, for he made no effort to escape them, except to rear up and paw the air half-heartedly before dropping his legs to the ground again and standing with lowered head, jaws apart, sucking in air.

The gauchos surrounded him. He looked from one to another with fear-filled eyes, feeling the sudden heat of the three sweating horses all about him, longing for the closeness of his dam. In that moment, for all his proud independence as a nine-month-old, he felt very young and lost and afraid.

Santiago and Miguel dismounted. Miguel tied a rope round the colt's hind legs while Santiago held one foreleg off the ground so that he could not kick himself free and, even though the colt was big now, his struggles to escape were in vain. Miguel jerked him to the ground and then tied his front legs to his hind legs while Santiago sat on his flank to keep him down. When this was done they left him alone to struggle frantically but hopelessly, wriggling like a fish out of water, kicking all fours at once spasmodically, unable to rise.

Vicente all this while was watching out for La Bruja. She had halted in the distance, aware at last that her foal was no longer following her, and she heard his desperate, frightened cries.

Great was her distress. She whinnied shrilly, pacing back and forth with tossing head, but even greater was her fear of man, so that she was prepared to sacrifice her foal before herself. The gauchos watched her together, having no compassion for the captive foal, wondering whether La Bruja would come to him or not.

La Bruja could not decide what to do. Her fear of mankind urged her to escape while she could, but her maternal instincts pulled her toward her helpless foal and his constant, plaintive cries were torture to her.

"Let's leave him here and go back to the horses," suggested Miguel. "She'll never come while she sees us near. We might take her unawares in the early morning. She'll come back to him tonight if he's alone."

La Bruja saw them mount their horses and ride away. She waited cautiously but with impatience until they were no more than midgets in the distance. By this time the foal had stopped crying and kicking, but lay exhausted and without hope where the gauchos had left him, hearing his mother's voice but having not the energy to answer it.

The rain had stopped, but the ground where the black colt lay was churned with mud from his struggles and the hoofprints of the other horses. He was a wretched creature in his helplessness, eyes staring and white-rimmed, and La Bruja when she came to him could do nothing but comfort him.

She nuzzled his flank and neck, sniffed at the ropes round his fetlocks and drew back with a snort of fear and disgust, smelling the scent of man. The colt began kicking and fighting again as he regained his strength, but nothing he could do was to any avail. The leather hobbles were strong and unbreakable and he fell back into the mud again with a heavy sigh, panting through open jaws. La Bruja tried to chew through the hobbles, but she was greatly hampered by the foal, who would not keep his legs still when she touched him.

Eventually La Bruja realized that she could do nothing for her youngling but stand beside him, and the moon gave her a long shadow on the pampa grass as it passed above her. She stood guard over the colt throughout the night, her whole body alert as she listened for the advent of the gauchos once again. More rain fell, a drab drizzle that had no ending, and the moon grew pale then vanished in the clouds.

With the coming of dawn La Bruja heard the rapid hoofbeats of the gauchos' horses once more and with a wild neigh of mingled fear and despair she deserted her post beside the captive colt and fled again before they could come upon her. The gauchos gave chase, but they could not catch her and another day passed as the first, with La Bruja for ever on the horizon, hardly visible in the rain, listening to her youngling's feeble cries.

She ventured close again at dusk, stalking warily toward the inert form of the colt, but her quick ears caught the sound of a horse spurting suddenly forward and she leaped away again with great speed. It was too dark for Vicente to throw his boleadoras with any accuracy and the fast spinning balls of stone missed La Bruja's legs in the grass. He gave up the chase, but

La Bruja was too afraid to return to her colt that night, knowing that the men had set a trap for her.

Several days passed in this fashion. La Bruja constantly circled about the place where the foal lay helpless, calling to him, but having not the courage to draw near. The gauchos chased her whenever she came close enough to make it worth their while, but never could they catch her, for she was too swift and nervous. It rained all the time and the skies were gray and black with masses of low clouds.

The gauchos tired of chasing after a creature so elusive as La Bruja, for it seemed impossible for them to capture her. Santiago was unwilling to try further, preferring to find work with some sure reward at the end of it. Miguel, his companion, said the same, so that Vicente had no alternative but to surrender her too. But Santiago had no intention of leaving empty-handed. He loosed the black colt and tethered him to his bell-mare, certain that he would make a fine mount once he was grown, and Vicente went to the home of El Ciego as he had originally planned, to tell him of La Bruja's return.

When the three men had gone, and La Bruja made sure that they had really gone and were not deceiving her any more, the lonely mare came back to where her colt had been lying. She sniffed all round the place, blankly, not understanding, and grief filled her as for days she hardly moved from where he had been.

She could not easily forget her spirited son, torn so harshly from her, and for a long time she moped and cried out her sadness, heard only by the vizcachas and the armadillo as they rambled nocturnally from place to place.

Eventually La Bruja forgot her grief, but in her heart her fading resentment against mankind was fired again and she was filled with new bitterness.

Chapter 18

ANGEL

I

It was soon after this that Angel came to know La Bruja. He had known of her for some time because, although too young to visit the barber's shop, being only ten years old, he knew most of the men who went there and they were only too glad to delight the young boy with new tales.

Angel was an orphan. No one knew his real name, nor even who his parents were, and he lived where he had been found, where someone had mysteriously left him as a ten-month-old baby one hot summer night, at the little adobe church on the pampa outside the town.

Father Orlando, the church's only occupant, found him lying on the porch, wrapped in an old gray poncho but otherwise naked, and, even though it was a close and sultry night, the babe was sleeping like an angel, his tiny sallow face content beneath a mop of straight black hair, and so the old priest named him.

Reluctant to surrender him to anyone in the town, the priest, after making vain enquiries for his parents, decided to look after him and no one really knew how he reared the little creature alone in his church, for it seemed a strange task for a priest. Angel thrived, however, and it was not until he had made his first attempts

to walk that Father Orlando discovered that he was
lame.

His left leg was slightly shorter than his right, but
he seemed to be a boy who could overcome all diffi-
culties. He learned to hop about quite well, clinging to
the scanty furniture in the priest's quarters and holding on to the fence of the corral outside where a pair
of horses and an old mule lived, until one of the gauchos who came to the church made him a little crutch
so that he could be more independent.

With this Angel was content. As he grew, he became
able to help the old Father with his many tasks, ringing the bell on Sundays and saints' days, taking feed
to the occupants of the corral, dusting the altar with
its figure of the Virgin—the only decoration the tiny
church possessed—replacing the candles when they
burned down and melting the remains to make new
ones. In one way and another he was fully occupied.
Father Orlando taught him to read and write and when
there was no task to be done Angel would take a book
and sit in the sun or in the shadow of the porch, read-
ing until he fell asleep and was carried to bed by the
priest.

Few people from town came to the church, for they
had their own church to go to, a larger, more splendid
place, while that on the pampa was hardly more than a
hermitage from whose rafters wild birds chattered and
flew during the service. It was a place of worship for
the gauchos. Too ashamed to enter the fine town
church in their rough clothes, hardly daring to tie
their half-wild ponies beside the superior carriage
horses of the town's gentry, the little adobe church on

the pampa satisfied their needs whenever they felt the urge to confess their sins or listen to the kindly advice of Father Orlando.

Angel's presence there was an added attraction and often they came just to talk to him and to tell him stories, bringing him at times strange pets: birds with broken wings, a harmless snake, an armadillo caught unawares; anything to make him smile. Seeing him hopping from place to place, dangling his useless leg, they came to know him affectionately as Ranito—Little Frog—and only the priest called him Angel or Angelito.

Angel first heard the story of La Bruja when he was eight and he followed it with interest, as did all the boys, both on the pampa and in the town, but for Angel she was more than just a renegade horse that had killed a man.

Unable to move at any pace faster than his customary hop, he was entranced by the glory of her speed, wondering what it must feel like to know no boundary of movement, to be freer than the freest horse because of her prowess.

When he was younger he had gazed wistfully at the boys brought by their parents to church, seeing them run and jump and somersault, and he had cried when alone to know that he could never do anything so normal. As he grew older he had learned to accept his limitations, finding contentment in smaller things, especially in the injured creatures brought to him by the gauchos, but many times he thought of La Bruja, seeing her gallop across the pampa in his imagination, following her in his heart with all her swiftness, hoping she would never be captured.

Angel was a lonely boy and wise for his years. Though he had known only ten summers, he had passed all this time in the company of Father Orlando, a kindly man but one too old to remember the desires and torments and the childish things of boyhood. He spoke to Angel as a contemporary and gave him serious, religious books to read, and Angel, a gentle, thoughtful boy because of his upbringing, never thought to question his mode of life, even though he sometimes longed for something different.

His whole world was the tiny church with its yellow ochre walls, thatched roof and big black doors carved with birds and animals and flowers by some unknown artist. The floor of the church was of stone, brought at some distant period from the southern lands, and the narrow porches on either side were stone-flagged too, giving added coolness to its shade. At some little distance from the church was a post, erected to look something like a gallows, and from this hung the bell with its dangling rope which Angel dutifully pulled every Sunday and on every special occasion.

In the rear of the church, behind the altar, Father Orlando and Angel each had a little room, bare, cell-like places, each with a cross above its narrow bed, and it was here that Angel dreamed mostly about La Bruja. She had hardly left his thoughts since he had first heard about her and sometimes he talked to the old Father about her.

"Father, do you think that God can see her?" he asked one day, his serious dark eyes watching the old man's weather-tanned face intently.

"Of course, my child. His eyes are everywhere."

"But do you think He cares?"

"He sees even when the sparrow falls."

"But when it has fallen," replied Angel impatiently to this obscure answer. "What happens when it has fallen? Would He save La Bruja from being caught or injured? I don't want her to be caught."

The child's earnestness made the priest realize how closely he held the savage horse to his heart and he could guess too that one day, and one day soon, La Bruja's fate must be resolved, probably brutally. He could not tell Angel that she would be safe, for he knew that she was in danger and that only a miracle could protect her from her enemies.

"We don't always get what we want, Angel, but that does not mean that God doesn't care. Sometimes a father must say no and, after all, this La Bruja you talk about has killed a man. We will see what happens to her."

With that reply Angel had to be satisfied, although he was far from happy. He had heard of her return to the district and that El Ciego wanted her. If La Bruja should be caught it would be the end of a dream for him, the end of an idea, for she was the embodiment of his desire to walk and run like normal boys.

He prayed for La Bruja every night and begged that she should be spared, little knowing then that it would be soon within his power to save her.

II

Angel was positive that it was design and not accident that made La Bruja come to the church, for if she had not come El Ciego would have caught her and there was no knowing what might have happened to her then. She might have refused to accept his mastery; she might have died or she might have killed again. But instead of any of these things she was safe in the church and Angel knew that it was an answer to his prayers.

He had known on the morning of the day that she came that El Ciego intended to capture her then. Some gauchos came riding by the day before and stopped to tell him the news, saying that the horse-breeder had arranged a large ambush for her, employing some forty men spread out over a wide distance to catch her. They had orders not to return until they had run her down and he had offered two of his best stallions to the man who finally ensnared her in his boleadoras or dropped a lasso over her head.

"She hasn't a chance of escape," said one, and it seemed as though there were a shade of regret in his voice.

"She must escape," replied Angel fervently. "She just mustn't be caught. When are they starting out?"

"Tomorrow morning, early. They know more or less where she is and reckon that by nightfall at the latest she'll be in their hands. Alive or dead, who can tell? But one way or another tomorrow is her last day of freedom."

They called for Father Orlando to give them his blessing before riding on and when they had gone Angel felt very lonely. It was as if his last hope in life had been dashed and he was so afraid for the solitary mare, feeling for her as if he had long possessed and loved her.

Father Orlando saw his misery and put his arm about the young boy's shoulders.

"Do not despair yet, Angelito. Have faith in your prayers—yes, I know you've prayed for her. Have faith and perhaps tomorrow your prayers will be answered."

Angel spent the whole of the following day out of doors. It was sunny but cold and he wore a poncho over his jacket—the latter the cast-off from some town boy—sitting on the corral fence most of the time so that he should be able to see a little farther.

For a long time he heard and saw nothing except the usual birds swooping up and down and calling to one another. The sky was heavy with white clouds, which at times threatened to extinguish the bright-blue patches in between and the grass looked green and fresh unto the horizon.

Angel did not know that La Bruja would run toward the church. She might equally well run in the opposite direction and then he could wait all day watching for her and see nothing. While he sat and waited and strained his eyes, Father Orlando busied himself by sweeping out the church. He had the big black doors wide open and he left them thus while he went to prepare a meal in order that the interior might be freshly aired.

He called Angel in to eat and the boy reluctantly surrendered his seat on the fence for half an hour, hopping anxiously back again as soon as Father Orlando gave him leave, half afraid that he might have missed something.

He waited until the sky was shadowed with coming dusk before any sounds came to his ears and then he heard distant, excited yells, the weary baying of over-taxed dogs, and he knew with a sudden leap of his heart that La Bruja was coming his way. Still he could see nothing, for the pampa was dark in the distance, but after what seemed an age he saw the dark shape of a fast racing horse and knew that it must be La Bruja.

Great was his excitement and great was his fear. He could see that she was exhausted. Her jaws hung open and as she drew nearer he could hear the terrible rasp of her empty lungs. He knew that she could run no further. At any moment she would drop in her tracks, drained completely of strength, and Angel could not bear to see her taken thus.

She ran blindly in her exhaustion, for if not, she could not have failed to see Angel sitting on the fence. So intent was the boy upon watching her that for the moment he had forgotten the existence of the hunters who came so closely behind. He was suddenly aware of them again as they whooped their excitement loudly and each man strained to overtake the other so that he might be able to claim the reward.

Angel stared at them. He saw that El Ciego was in the lead. He knew it was he, for he rode his favorite palomino stallion, the magnificent Eldorado, famed in the district, and no other man had a horse like that. For the first time in his life Angel felt hatred. As he loved and pitied La Bruja, so he hated and despised those who chased her, and he sat almost paralyzed on the fence watching pursued and pursuers, unable to do anything to help the one or hinder the others.

Many times Angel thought of La Bruja, seeing her gallop across the pampa.

It was then that the miracle happened, or so Angel considered it to be.

La Bruja, dashing past Angel with bloodshot eyes, spraying him with foam from her gasping jaws, darted directly into the church and he could hear her hoofs clattering over the flagstones as she blundered in the dark. Perhaps she had not intended to hide there, perhaps she had not even seen the open doors but ran blindly through them because the church was in her path. Whatever the reason, Angel acted instantly. He jumped from the fence, grabbed his crutch, and hopped faster than he had ever done in his life to close the doors before she could get out or before El Ciego could get in.

He closed them only just in time. The horse-breeder drew his panting stallion to a rearing halt beside the doors and demanded that Angel open them again.

"No."

"What do you mean by no?" contested El Ciego angrily. "That's my horse in there and I want her."

"She's not your horse," retorted Angel boldly. "She doesn't belong to anyone and she's taken shelter in the church of her own free will. You can't drive her out and I won't turn her out."

"Why, you . . ."

At that moment Father Orlando, hearing all the commotion, came hurrying to find out what had happened. He saw the snorting, sweating horses and the angry horse-breeder, all being defied by the small but angry boy who stood before the carven doors, and he called out: "What's the matter? What do all you people want?"

El Ciego turned his horse about and guided him toward the priest.

"Father Orlando, I'm glad to see you," he greeted the old man. "Perhaps you will do what this boy refuses. A mare we were chasing has taken refuge in the church and I'd be grateful if you'd open the doors and let her out."

Father Orlando summed up the situation instantly. He saw Angel's flushed, excited face, eyes bright with hope, fervent in the belief that his prayers had been answered; and he saw the angry horse-breeder who was proud and haughty and thought he had a right to possess anything he desired.

He answered calmly, gazing up at the angry man. "My friend, if, to use your own expression, the horse has taken refuge in the church I can't drive it out. Obviously the creature came seeking sanctuary and I cannot deny it."

El Ciego snorted angrily.

"Sanctuary! How can a horse have sanctuary? Only men can demand that."

"In my church there is sanctuary for all who seek it," replied the old priest softly.

"How do you know she was seeking sanctuary then?" asked El Ciego, trying to change his tactics. "She dashed into the church and this boy shut the doors so that she couldn't escape. Open them again. If she comes out she's mine."

"And if she stays?" asked Father Orlando.

El Ciego snorted again, this time with amusement.

"She won't stay, Father Orlando. She doesn't know what sanctuary is."

Father Orlando made no reply. Instead he gazed steadily at Angel and said: "Open the doors, Angel. We'll see if she understands or not."

Angel hesitated, fearing to do as he was commanded in case La Bruja should dash out again. He returned the old man's gaze and saw understanding in his eyes. Obviously the priest had more faith than he did. He turned to the doors, grasped the huge handle and pulled.

In the church all was silent. Angel waited breathlessly, El Ciego expectantly. Only Father Orlando seemed unmoved by any emotion. It was as if he knew what the outcome would be.

In the darkness of the little church, panting heavily as she lay on the cold, white flagstones, La Bruja did not stir as the fading daylight entered. She did not care where she was. It was still and calm and instinctively she felt that no one would molest her. Here was sanctuary at last and she was unafraid.

Chapter 19

A LEGEND DIES

I

El Ciego was not a man to give in easily, especially when his pride was at stake. He had told everyone that he would own La Bruja and when the news should reach the town that the crippled church boy refused to part with her he would be the butt of many jokes. Therefore he returned again to the church, this time intending to use persuasion, and he took with him the two stallions promised to the man who captured La Bruja. He regretted parting with the beasts, but if it were to gain La Bruja it would be worth it.

Two days had passed when he returned and in that time Angel and Father Orlando, with the help of a gaucho favorably disposed toward them, had managed to get La Bruja into the corral. This was not without a struggle for she was savage with fear and could not be approached. Father Orlando refused to allow Angel near her, even though he was unafraid and had wanted to take food to her on her first night in the church.

"She's a killer, Angelito. She might attack you if you venture near her. No, we must leave her for the night and decide what can be done with her tomorrow."

"But she'll be hungry," protested the boy.

"She won't die."

Father Orlando's usually serene face was troubled. To keep La Bruja in the church for an indefinite period was impossible and he had grave doubts about allowing her to stay there in the first place. There was no denying the fact that she was defiling his church, however unwittingly, and he could hardly perform future services and listen to confessions in the presence of a horse. But how to get her out of the church without losing her? She would surely fall into the hands of El Ciego if she were free.

With these problems on his mind he said gravely to Angel, "You know we can't keep her, don't you?"

"Why not, Father Orlando? I'll look after her."

"How, my son? To keep her you must tame her."

"I'll do that, too. I'll tame her by being kind to her. Then she'll grow to trust me."

"Well, we'll see," replied Father Orlando to Angel's hopeful remarks. "We must first remove her from the church before we decide upon anything else."

This problem was solved by Alfredo, a young gaucho who lived nearby and who had come to see La Bruja, for he had heard that she had taken sanctuary in the church. He was quite fond of the old priest, having known him all his life, and all three of his young children had been baptized by him. He lived with his family in a small adobe house not more than ten miles away and was one of Father Orlando's regular visitors.

The priest explained the problem to him, and Alfredo, who had no particular wish to see the horse-breeder possess yet another unusual animal, said: "I could lasso her for you and drag her to the corral. That should be easy enough. Open the doors and as she runs out I'll drop a rope over her head."

"Are you sure you won't miss?" asked Angel doubtfully.

"Don't worry. I've been roping cattle and horses for years."

So they did as Alfredo suggested. They opened one door only and they heard the rush of La Bruja's hoofs on the stones as she darted for freedom after being locked in the church for so long. She had regained much of her lost strength, enough to make her angry and wild again, and they had heard her neighing and clattering about all morning, blundering clumsily into things as she tried to find a way out by herself. When daylight suddenly flooded the church she was startled, but needed only a second to realize that beyond the doorway was freedom.

She dashed through the open door, blinded momentarily by the light which flashed into her eyes after the obscurity of the church, whose candles had burned out overnight. She felt the rope settle about her neck and she reared up with a scream of rage, attacking it with her fore-hoofs and startling Angel, who had not thought her so wild.

Alfredo jerked the rope tight. He was astride his pony when he lassoed her and it was only the work of a few minutes to drag her struggling to the corral where Father Orlando stood beside the open gate. The gaucho pulled her half choking into the corral, then slackened the rope as he hastily backed his pony out.

Feeling the rope's looseness, La Bruja tossed her head and shook her neck, pawing at it until she man-

aged to throw the rope off. Then she glared balefully
at the three people watching her, unaware of their kind
intentions toward her. She made a hasty examination of
the corral, ignoring its inmates, although they stared at
her in curiosity but did not dare to approach her. She
sniffed at the rails, grunting impatiently and with anger,
pricking and flattening her ears, and she was all nerv-
ousness in her actions, rolling her eyes, ringing her
tail, never still for one moment.

"Let's leave her in peace, Angel," suggested Father
Orlando eventually. "We must allow her time to settle
before trying to overcome her antagonism toward us."

"Would you like me to try to break her for you?"
said Alfredo to Angel.

"No, no. I don't want her broken," replied the boy
hastily. "Please just leave her alone. I'll tame her my
own way."

So they left her alone and when they had gone, having discovered that there was no way out of the corral,
La Bruja stood in one corner, trembling and stamping
a hoof until she remembered that she was hungry.
Then she began to snatch at the grass which grew in
patches round the sides of the corral, lifting her head
every few moments to watch for any sign of impend-
ing danger. None came and eventually she grew calmer.

Thus El Ciego discovered her when he came riding
up to the church once again, trailing the stallions behind him. Angel saw him coming and called to Father
Orlando, so that together they awaited him, neither of
them trusting him very much.

"She's not in sanctuary now, Father," called out El
Ciego in a bantering tone as he approached.

"The corral is church property," replied the old priest firmly. "If you remove her from it you will be breaking the eighth commandment."

"I haven't come to steal, Father. Look, I've brought with me two fine stallions for the boy, the very same I promised to whosoever should catch the mare."

Angel stared at the stallions. A well-matched pair, they were both chestnut in color. One had a white star on his forehead and the other a white blaze. They snorted and pranced back and forth, spirited creatures, nibbling and biting each other, both friendly and animus at the same time.

"What do you think of them, boy?" said El Ciego, seeing Angel's admiring gaze.

"They're beautiful."

"Wouldn't you like to own them?"

"What would I do with them?"

"What will you do with La Bruja?"

"I don't know yet, but I know I shan't exchange her for the stallions."

With difficulty El Ciego kept his anger in check. The boy was too quick for him, his insolent replies veiled in politeness.

"What will you exchange her for, then?"

Angel thought. Then he grinned as he stared up at the horse-breeder who held with a tight rein the impatient palomino he always rode.

"Eldorado," he said.

At this reply El Ciego looked incredulous and could no longer contain his anger.

"Don't be a fool, boy," he shouted. "You know I will never part with this horse."

"Well, that's how much I value La Bruja," said Angel. "I shall never sell her or exchange her for anything."

II

Alfredo was not the only man to call to see La Bruja. Very soon there came a steady stream of gauchos and townfolk, ostensibly to visit the church, who always stopped at the corral first and might well have ridden away again had not Father Orlando come out to greet them. Even the fat barber came, although his story had lost some of its interest because La Bruja was not fabulous at all but just an ugly, angry mare. Those who had not seen her run could find no words to praise her and the legend of her exploits faded and died now that she had been captured and seen at close quarters.

Father Orlando took advantage of the interested callers, welcoming them to his church in all innocence, as if he did not know that they had come only to see La Bruja. He knew they would not come again, so that he took advantage of his opportunity to stir their consciences while he could.

El Ciego did not return, knowing that Angel was adamant, but he told his men to keep an eye on the horse and let him know how Angel progressed with her. Perhaps she might escape him one day if he tried to ride her and then he would make sure that he did not lose her a second time.

Although Father Orlando enjoyed all the unexpected visitors and gained the promise of several to come to his church more regularly in the future, Angel was dismayed. La Bruja hardly knew a moment's peace in the corral, for nearly every day someone came to gaze at her, while on Sundays she was worked almost to a frenzy of rage.

He would not have minded so much if they had been content just to look at her, then leave her alone, but they were not. One young fellow tried to ride her, jumping upon her back from the fence while another attracted her attention. She twisted and turned like a whirlwind and flung him to the ground, crashing her hoofs down beside his skull in an effort to destroy him, and Angel, for all his gentleness, was almost sorry that she missed.

He himself had little opportunity to find La Bruja alone. His plan had been to let her come to him and he wanted to do no more than sit on the corral fence and watch her until she no longer looked upon him as a foe. But so fearful and enraged was she by all the men who stared at her, shouted at her and tried to touch her that Angel's effort was in vain. He came to her at dusk, long after the last visitor had gone away but, overexcited and angered by the day's events, La Bruja looked upon him only as another tormentor and either escaped to the other end of the corral or tried to attack him.

Angel hardly expected the way to La Bruja's heart to be a stoneless one and he was prepared to use endless patience in order to gain her trust, but in everything he was frustrated because he could not have La Bruja alone. He complained to Father Orlando, but there was little comfort in the priest's counsel of patience when he said that very soon La Bruja would be forgotten and the men would come no more to see her. She was being ruined now, when it was most important that she should gain confidence, and Angel was in torment for her because of the unnecessary suffering she was forced to endure. No wonder she was savage and hated mankind.

Father Orlando's prophecy, assisted by the weather, came true. There followed a time of heavy, enduring rain when hardly a soul ventured to cross the pampa unless he had good cause, and when the rain had ceased and the sun shone once more it seemed that La Bruja was forgotten, for no one came to see her. Angel rejoiced. He himself had not gone near her except to take her bundles of grass, so that for almost a fortnight LaBruja was unmolested, alone except for her three companions, whom still she ignored.

When the rain ceased Angel recommenced his plan. He had all the time in the world and did not despair when La Bruja showed no signs of gladness at his presence. As soon as he was free of his lessons and had done his daily tasks, he hopped to the corral and sat on the fence, talking to the mare with coaxing voice, not venturing any nearer to her both of his own accord and at the instructions of Father Orlando, who did not trust her.

He grew not to see her ugliness, for he loved her and was satisfied just to have her near enough to visit every day. He knew that she mistrusted him because of her past ill treatment and felt sure that soon she would come to accept him as a friend. Because he loved her he wanted her to return his feeling and his greatest desire was to have that pink, damp muzzle touching his hands of its own accord, to be able to stroke that ugly head. He found it difficult to concentrate on his lessons, but Father Orlando understood his restlessness and chided him only gently, at times telling him to go to La Bruja and talk to her until he was ready to come to his books again.

Thus the days and weeks passed by, but Angel grew no nearer to the affections of La Bruja, although she gradually lost her fear of him and did not dart to the other end of the corral at his approach. He never attempted to touch her, resisting his frequent impulse to do so, waiting for her to make the first move.

He waited in vain. She stared at him, but seemed disinterested in his voice. She looked at his out-stretched hands and then ignored them. She spent much of her time, when not eating, just gazing over the fence, her chin resting on the top bar, pricking her ears as birds chattered and flew overhead but other-wise listless.

Sometimes she saw a gaucho ride by at a gallop and her body would tremble as if preparing for flight, then she would relax again. On Sundays she was always rest-less, for that was the one day when people always came to the church, not many but those who came stopped at the corral to look at La Bruja and comment on her and the boys would try to make her run and jump, startling her with a variety of noises, much to Angel's annoyance.

He would watch them while pulling the bell-rope, longing to yell out, but knowing that Father Orlando would not approve, and when the service was over and everyone had departed he would hurry to the corral and talk to La Bruja in a soothing voice, hoping she would understand that he wanted to help her, hoping she would feel his love. If she did she made no sign and the best he could expect was that she would not shy away.

Angel often wondered about the halter round her head. Had it been put there by the young man of whom the barber spoke, or was it the mark of some other owner? He wanted to remove it because he wanted La Bruja to be free of the trappings of man, undominated, and this was a conflict within him, for, although he was glad to have La Bruja in his hands, he had always imagined her free like the birds and even now she represented the power he did not possess.

He wanted to know that she might race across the pampa still, but not at the command of a master. He wanted her tame and yet he wanted her wild and he knew that he could not have both.

Chapter 20

THE ONLY WAY

I

Spring was coming to the pampa once again. The summer birds winged across the land once more, shadowing the pampa beneath them, and La Bruja trembled with frustrated eagerness as they flew above the corral where still she was a prisoner, recognizing the season and longing for her freedom.

Angel knew and understood her mood. She had come to accept his friendship at last, permitting herself to be stroked and handled, remembering perhaps her Indian master, but she gave little affection in return. She no longer bared her teeth and flattened her ears at his approach she no longer shied away, but she never came to him of her own accord, she never sought his friendship, accepting it only because she realized that he meant her no harm.

As a prisoner she was miserable. Her life with Onak had made her restless, but at least with him she could run out her fever for freedom. With Angel, who had never tried to ride her, she had nothing to do but stand in the corral or wander round it time and time again, occasionally brushing noses with the other occupants. She passed the time staring over the fence, watching, listening and smelling, and when spring came again her listless heart was stirred, forgotten instincts were aroused and the fast flying birds called to her with tormenting insistence. Follow, follow, was what they cried to her, but she was halted by a stubborn fence.

Angel saw and felt her restlessness. He had studied her closely in his love throughout the months she had been in his keeping and he knew her well. He knew exactly how she tossed her head and pawed the ground, impatient for the feed he brought her; he knew when she was irritable or sleepy or when she had found a sudden interest in something; he knew that she did not love him, that her heart was too wild ever to accept the domination of man, whether kind or cruel, that she was unhappy in her captivity, and many times he wanted to release her, held back only by the knowledge that El Ciego was still waiting for her. He removed the halter from her head, but still he could not give her freedom.

As he came to understand La Bruja he realized that she was no killer born. True she was wild, true she was savage, but once he had conquered her fear, and let her understand that he would not harm her, he saw that she was quiet and honest. She played him no mean tricks, her vicious eyes became more gentle, and now she rarely flattened her ears. Only fear or cruelty could have driven her to kill the man, and Angel told this to every gaucho who came to church longing to clear her name, for there were still those who said she should be destroyed for what she had done.

They were surprised to learn that he had tamed her, but they had the word of Father Orlando that it was true, even though she grew anxious and angry when

other men came to look at her. After a while some men
began to remember that Gregorio had always been impatient with horses, agreeing that perhaps La Bruja
had been too much provoked. Angel cleared her name
and the fat town barber lost his favorite story.

Angel tried to ignore La Bruja's restless spirit, knowing that he could not let her free even though he
longed to make her happy, for in his love he was un-
selfish and did not wish to keep her against her will.
How much he hoped that she would come to return
his affection, how often he dreamed that one day he
would open the gate of the corral and that she would
not venture through it, only to awake and tell himself
that she would in reality dash away without a moment's hesitation.

While he gained her trust the winter slowly passed
away and he saw that each day nearer to the spring
La Bruja grew more restless, newly searching for a
weak spot in the corral, although she had long ago
given up any hope of escape.

"Father Orlando, what can I do?" he begged one
day. "I want to let her free and yet I know I mustn't."

"Well, Angelito, you can let her free. She will run
away and know perhaps ten days of happiness before
she's captured once again. Or you can keep her until
she's old and has gray whiskers on her muzzle like
the others, knowing that she isn't happy but that she's
well looked after."

"Ten days of happiness against a lifetime of misery.
Which would I choose if it were me?" said Angel. "But
if she has the ten days then there will be a lifetime

with El Ciego afterward, from whom we've already saved her, or some other man she hates as much."

"Perhaps, perhaps not," replied the priest. "She's your horse, Angel my son. You must solve the problem, make the choice for her. You know her so well that you should know which she would choose."

Angel said nothing to this. He knew well enough which she would choose, but he could not bear to think of her in another man's possession. He was this much selfish in his love for her. He must have her or she must be free completely. He would not give her to another man.

He sat on the fence and watched her, for the first time in his life facing a seemingly unanswerable problem. He remembered how he had first seen her—a beaten, exhausted creature with bloodshot eyes and choking breath. He remembered how he had always visualized her, galloping with eager legs and wind-blown tail, eyes shining with delight. He saw her now with drooping head and lifeless eyes, and the only thought that gave him gladness was the one in which he saw her free.

II

Angel saw the payador from a distance, recognizing him by the guitar across his shoulders and the horse he rode, and he hurried to tell Father Orlando of his coming, his troubled heart gladdened by the thought of the old man's company, for he could tell tales of fantasy such as never were found in his religious books and sing songs far more exciting than hymns.

The payador rode a horse which had long been El Ciego's envy. A bronze-coated, black-legged mare she was and the horse-breeder felt sure that she could foal a polomino colt by Eldorado. Many times had he offered the old man money or horses in exchange for her, but the payador would not part with Thamár, talking of her as if she were a daughter instead of just a horse. When he told El Ciego that the wild La Bruja was her mother it was because he knew that El Ciego would desire her more and, like many a man, he enjoyed saying no to the horse-breeder.

The payador came to the church for two reasons. One was that he had long neglected his religion and wanted to talk to Father Orlando, and the other reason was that he had too had heard of La Bruja's presence there and wished to see the ugly mother of his beautiful Thamár once more.

La Bruja did not know her daughter. Thamár was unsaddled and turned loose in the corral, and La Bruja, in curiosity, examined her and then ignored her, having long forgotten that she had borne colt and filly on the pampa, no longer remembering her grief at their loss. Angel gazed with interest and admiration at the lovely creature, filled with pride to think that she could be the daughter of La Bruja, but his heart grew heavy when he learned from the payador how El Ciego still thought to gain his mare, delight fading from his sun-browned face.

"What's the matter, Ranito?" asked the payador. "Are you afraid that he will steal her?"

"No. I know he won't do that. At least, he would not steal her from me. He would steal her from the pampa, though, where she belongs. Even I don't really own her."

"Tell me about her," the payador urged the serious, sad-eyed boy, as eager to hear stories as to tell them, and Angel gazed into his sympathetic, understanding eyes and knew that here he had a friend.

Gladly he poured out his troubles, unburdening himself as he did so, feeling sure that the payador could help him. He saw how Thamár loved her master, he saw how gently he treated her, how he chided her and spoke to her and called her "friend." For a moment he was even willing to give La Bruja to him, knowing that he would treat mother and daughter alike, but he told the payador, "I want her to be free."

They leaned against the corral fence together, the warm spring sunshine beating down upon them from an azure sky, and Father Orlando joined them, saying nothing but listening to the boy, never realizing until this moment just how much Angel had worried and hoped and feared. The payador said nothing either, only nodding now and again until the boy had finished.

Then he said, "There's only one answer to your problem, Ranito, only one thing to do and you can only do it if you really love La Bruja because it's something very hard."

"I do love her, I do, and I'd do anything for her," Angel vowed. "Tell me what I must do."

"To let her free you must take away that which makes her coveted by other men."

Angel said nothing to this, not understanding.

He frowned and thought and the payador left him to think, knowing that soon he would comprehend. Angel suddenly stared at the old gaucho, disbelief in his innocent, black eyes as he understood.

"You mean take away her speed? Cripple her?"

The payador nodded, returning Angel's gaze.

"But that's cruel. How could I do it without hurting her? How could she ever trust me again?"

"You cannot do it without hurting her, but once you let her free you won't need her to trust you. Sometimes it's necessary to be cruel in order to be kind, surely you can understand that?"

Angel made no reply, struggling to fit this new idea with all the others he had entertained. Never in his life would he hurt La Bruja, that he knew, and yet the payador was telling him that he must, and hurt her cruelly, if he really wanted to prove his love for her. He knew the despair of being lame, never able to do the things he wanted, and must La Bruja suffer thus and at his hands?

"Is there no other way?" he pleaded at last, looking from one man to the other, seeing the answer in both their eyes.

"The payador is wise," said Father Orlando. "You would do well to listen to him."

"You must do that or keep her for ever. There is no other way," added the payador, and Angel knew he was right.

He sighed and looked at La Bruja, knowing how she strained every nerve in her longing to be free, and he wondered how highly she valued her freedom or whether her love of running was greater. He guessed that the two would be combined and he realized that if he chose he could give her one thing or neither. No matter how much he desired it, he could not give her both.

"Very well," he said at last to the payador. "But you do it, señor, because I cannot. I love her too much to hurt her."

"She won't let me near her, Ranito, you know that. You must do it because she trusts you, otherwise we will need ropes and more men to help us, which will only frighten her."

Angel nodded, his face pale and his eyes showing the strain of his heart. He felt sick with fear when the payador handed him his long silver knife, taking it gingerly, looking at it with distaste. He placed it in his own belt at last, thinking that La Bruja might be afraid if she saw it.

"Cut a back tendon," advised the payador. "In the pastern, just above the hoof. One quick stab is all you need but make it a strong one. She won't let you near her a second time."

Angel did not speak. He hopped slowly to the gate of the corral and stood there for several moments, his back to the men, but they could guess by his actions that he was rubbing tears from his face.

With a heavy heart he went up to La Bruja, stroking her gently as often he had done, unable to talk to her for the lump in his throat, hoping she would sense that he loved her, longing for her to understand what he was about to do. For a long time he paused, putting off the moment again and again, trying to make himself realize that once it was done she would never gallop again, that she would be without value to any man.

"Oh, Bruja, Bruja," he said to her at last. "Why wouldn't you come to love me? Why do you love freedom so much? Why is your heart so wild? We could have been great friends, you and I. Instead we shall be two cripples. Be happy on the pampa, ugly cripple. No man will ever want you again."

He leaned against her while he felt in his pocket, suddenly remembering the rosary of black wooden beads he always kept there. He pulled it out and took a piece of La Bruja's long, dark mane in his hands, firmly entwining the rosary among the wiry hairs, the only thing he had that he could give her. La Bruja shook her neck and snorted and then stood still again, sensing Angel's change of mood but not understanding it.

Then Angel took the knife from his belt and felt his way down La Bruja's off hind leg, letting his hand move slowly so that he should not frighten her. It was no easy job, for he was hampered by his crutch, and after a moment he threw the crutch aside and knelt in the dust beside La Bruja, unafraid, not even thinking that she might kick him. He forgot that the payador and Father Orlando were watching him, he forgot everything in that moment except that the deed must be done, and suddenly he filled his heart with courage and stabbed the point of the knife deep into the pastern as the payador had told him.

La Bruja jumped into the air, kicking savagely, squealing with sudden pain and Angel fell flat on his back as he dodged her hoofs, vaguely seeing her dart

across the corral and through the open gate, half
blinded by dust and tears.

He pulled himself to his knees and watched her, not
sure if he had lamed her or not, for she had jumped
away quickly enough and seemed to run without im-
pediment. He saw that the dust was damp with
blotches of blood and, as he tore his gaze from them
to stare again at La Bruja, he saw that she had faltered
in her stride, halting to touch her wounded fetlock
with her muzzle, unable to put her hoof to the
ground.

He had not failed and the tears he had so far
stemmed suddenly filled his eyes so that he could not
see her limping to freedom. He sobbed as if his heart
would break.

Angel never saw La Bruja again. The payador, when
he took his leave of the occupants of the little church,
rode to the rancho of El Ciego and told him what
Angel had done, and often after that, when called to
sing a song of the pampa, he would sing about La
Bruja.

Every now and then a gaucho coming to the church
would tell Angel that he had spied La Bruja from a
distance and thus the boy learned how she was far-
ing. The spring with its urgent messages passed away,
the hot summer too, during which time the thistles
grew, flowered and dropped their seeds; birds nested
and hatched their fledglings; storms refreshed the wilting grass and flowers. Another winter came and went
and a year passed by since Angel had kept La Bruja
in the corral.

Another gaucho came and said that he had seen the mare with a fine, dark colt and that she wandered along in the wake of a large herd led by a dun-colored stallion, and then there was no more news of her, for the herd passed from the district and La Bruja was not seen again.

Angel never forgot La Bruja. Even when he became a man and a priest, taking charge of the little church on the pampa when Father Orlando died, he still remembered the wild horse he had befriended and saved, staring at the now empty corral and wondering whether she had found her way to Trapalanda as he believed, for surely in Trapalanda La Bruja deserved to be.